Miestryri

A Dreg Novella

Bethany Hoeflich

Copyright © 2019 Bethany Hoeflich

All rights reserved. No part of this publication may be reproduced, distributed, or transmitted in any form or by any means including photocopying, recording, or other electronic or mechanical methods, without the prior written permission of the publishers, except in the case of brief quotations in reviews and certain other noncommercial uses permitted by copyright law.

This is a work of fiction. Any resemblance to actual persons, living or dead, is purely coincidental.

ISBN: 9781700507051

Cover Art by DwBookCovers

For Steel

*Who insisted on having
a book of his own*

1

It was a good day for a funeral.

The waves were still. Quiet. As if the sea itself were holding its breath in homage to a legend. Even the sky had cleared of clouds, leaving no blemish on the cerulean expanse. The morning sun glistened on the gentle waves as they lapped the curving shore. A small crowd, wearing the traditional white mourning clothes of Crystalmoor, had gathered on the pale sands of East Rock to pay their respects to the fallen Miestryri. More still were picking their way down the perilous staircase that had been carved into the cliffside. For many of them, it would be their first and last chance to see the fallen Miestryri with their own eyes.

But no matter how pious and respectful they appeared, the funeral had not drawn them to the beach like lemmings tumbling over the cliff. Nor had the dozen priests, bedecked in splendid ombre robes that began as white at their shoulders and darkened to the deep, gray-blue of an angry sea at their ankles. On their heads, they wore woven crowns of seaweed, and around their necks, strings of sea glass and shells that rattled as they moved like waves on bare feet, sinking into the dance of death to honor the fallen. It was a spectacle that would draw even the most critical eye with wonder, yet no one bothered to watch. Every eye, every gaze, was rooted to the figure waiting in the shadows of the cliff.

The exiled prince—long presumed dead—had returned.

Shaking off the weight of the crowd's speculative gaze as a horse shakes off the irritating sting of a fly, Prince Silvano Miore' watched the procession with his heart in his throat as the priests of the sea god carried his father's funeral raft past the sheer cliffs and down to the shoreline.

Any moment he expected to wake up and discover that this was nothing more than a nightmare.

Was it only yesterday that he had met with his father in the hopes of reconciling their differences?

It felt like a lifetime ago. Instead of the touching reunion he'd hoped for, his father had greeted him with an outstretched sword. With no other choice, Silvano was forced to defend himself. He'd cut his own father down like a spindly tree in the forest.

But the people wouldn't accept his explanation, even if he wished to give one. Even now, he heard their accusations—kin-killer. Their whispers followed him like feral dogs, nipping at his heels as he strode past the crowd. No matter what he said, they wouldn't accept his defense. In their mind, he was the banished prince. A playboy turned murderer. Disgraced beyond redemption.

And so he stayed silent, accepting their scorn like the sting of a whip in penance. Maybe then it would ease his guilt.

They didn't know that his own father had hired his Shield, Mikkal, to kill him after they crossed the border into Lingate—a task that Mikkal had failed, much to Silvano's relief. He very much enjoyed keeping his head attached to his neck where it belonged. While the betrayal still ate away at his mind like acid, the lesson it had taught him was invaluable. He would never again trust blindly.

Muffled footsteps drew near, interrupting his musings. Silvano took a deep breath before turning toward the approaching guard. Dressed in the official uniform of the royal guard, Jax cut an imposing figure in his tailored gray tunic and linen breeches. Due to superstition, few of the Crystalmoor guard would dare wear iron, but Jax wore the chest plate and shoulder guards with pride. Or possibly insanity. Flaunting his disregard for tradition in front of the priests at a funeral wasn't the wisest idea. His proud face was drawn in a frown, and his gaze traveled over the gathering crowd.

"Anything to report?" Silvano asked. Jax was one of his oldest friends, and it meant the world that he would support him without question, despite the rumors. And with a powerful Gifted at his back, Silvano could breathe easier knowing that his position, while tenuous at best, would be defended to the last.

Jax dipped his head and whispered, "Our counts show strong opposition, sire."

Silvano waved him off. "None of that formal nonsense. Speak freely."

"The majority would support Arianna if she challenged your claim." Jax winced and turned toward the sea, his eyes roving the crowd for a threat, whether real or perceived. "I see she's not here."

"No, she's not." His sister was the one person who would be an asset to his ascension, or a threat.

She was smart, charming, and she had a deep-rooted interest in the people's wellbeing. On top of that, she'd taken a keen interest in politics while Silvano had been out partying and womanizing.

A reputation he had earned only because people were too ignorant to see past their expectations.

Arianna's absence chafed. Why wasn't she here with the rest of the mourners? Their stepmother stood at the head of the procession, dressed in a white gown and veil, her arms wrapped around their half-sister, Lucinda. Even Lucan, his father's advisor, had been retrieved from the dungeon so he could pay his respects. But not Arianna.

Silvano eyed Lucan with barely-concealed hatred. He wanted nothing more than to throw him from the cliffs.

"Sire," Jax began, clearly reluctant to speak his thoughts, "we must consider the possibility that she's plotting against you."

"Enough. I will deal with my sister when she deigns to make an appearance. Tell me of the rest."

"A few would prefer to follow Aravell's lead and elect their own representatives. Only a handful will support your reign without question."

"So, we're in over our heads," he said, tapping his chin thoughtfully. He took a deep breath of the salty air, allowing it to cleanse him. "I've faced worse odds. I'll admit, it hasn't been quite the homecoming I'd imagined. Then again, what could I expect from a man who paid my own Shield to assassinate me."

Jax shuffled his boot in the sand. "Sil... what happened?" he asked, abandoning formality and letting their childhood familiarity shine through his words.

For a moment, Silvano was transported back to being ten years old, burying Jackson up to his neck in the sand on this very beach. The corner of his mouth tugged up in a smile as he remembered the whipping his father had given him when the tide came in and he hadn't freed his friend yet. Jax had spent the next week coughing up seawater but was otherwise no worse for wear.

His eyes landed on the Miestryri's funeral raft, and the reality of the situation slammed into him. They were no longer boys wasting time on the surf. The next few days would have far-reaching consequences on the security of his reign, and he couldn't afford to allow the past to distract him from the future. Silvano's jaw clenched, and he turned his face away, not wanting to see the judgment in Jax's eyes. "I do not wish to speak of it."

Maybe Jax picked up Silvano's tone and decided to drop the subject. Or maybe his sense of duty pulled his attention back to the growing crowd by the shore. Either way, he stopped pestering Silvano, for which he was grateful. If it weren't for the tell-tale tick in his jaw, and the way his eye twitched slightly, Silvano might have thought he hadn't heard him at all.

Silvano's eyes roved the crowd, hoping for a glimpse of one person in particular. He spotted her standing at the front, dabbing at her eyes with a handkerchief, with her new husband waiting at her side. Olielle. He swallowed thickly, trying to ignore the flare of acidic jealousy that bubbled up his gut. How quickly his betrothed had moved on in his absence.

As if she could feel his scrutiny, Olielle turned to look at him and their eyes locked. Silvano's heart skipped a beat. Though their relationship had never been romantic, he couldn't help but notice the way her golden skin sparkled, or how her deep auburn hair caught the sunlight just right. If he wished, he could still claim her. He shook his head to clear it. It was never meant to be.

The priest beckoned Silvano forward. His hand darted to the pocket of his white doublet where a single gold coin weighed heavier than a brick. Those who followed the sea god believed that a person was reincarnated according to their adherence to the old ways. While most had abandoned their beliefs, the superstitions remained. When someone died, they would place a coin on their tongues as payment for their new bodies when they were born into a new life. Silvano believed it was nonsense, but he wasn't willing to take that chance. How could he deny his father if it were true?

The crowd's murmurs grew louder as he stepped toward the sea—toward the Miestryri's funeral raft. In life, his father had seemed as great as a giant, but in death, his cheeks were sunken into his skull. Though the skin was stretched tight across his face, the perpetual scowl he'd always worn was absent, making him look peaceful. If only he'd been as stoic in real life.

Without waiting for further instruction, Silvano placed a palm on the dead ruler's chin, opened his mouth, and slipped a gold coin through his teeth to rest on his tongue. He closed his eyes, sending a wordless plea to the sea god in the hopes that the next life would be better than this one had been. While Silvano believed it was nonsense—his father's body was likely going nowhere but a hungry shark's stomach—catering to the beliefs of the people couldn't hurt.

Four priests stepped forward and took hold of the poles at each corner of the raft, lifting it to rest on their shoulders as they waded deeper into the water. In rich, baritone voices, they incanted, "From the sea we come, to the sea we return."

"We anoint his head with salt."

"We bathe his feet with foam."

"May the sea god guide his way to the depths of Paradisillo."

"Or return him with glory and honor, reborn."

The priests lowered the raft into the water, the waves crashing against it, threatening to overturn it in the sea. Silvano stepped forward so the water splashed against his boots. He lifted his hands and pushed, commanding the sea to take his father's body. A hush descended over the crowd as they observed his power, as he dared to claim a duty that should have been performed by a priest. It didn't feel right to leave such a personal task for the impersonal priests. If he couldn't reconcile with his father, the least he could do was honor him in this way.

The crowd was mercifully silent as the raft slipped beyond the reef. For all his faults, the Miestryri had maintained peace in Crystalmoor for the past thirty years. He had expanded trade with Kearar and Talos, and he'd protected the fleet from Belosian pirates. The people were safe, for now, and probably terrified of what would happen under the next Miestryri's rule.

When the raft was no more than a dark speck on the horizon, Silvano turned to the priests as they waded back to shore. It was time for him to claim his birthright. He tilted his chin upward and broke the silence. "I would have you anoint me now."

The eldest priest, with long, white hair that hung to his shoulder blades and a nose that could cut through paper, frowned at him. "Would you disrespect the dead?"

Silvano raised his voice to carry to the crowd. The priests wouldn't dare humiliate him in front of the people. "It is our custom for the successor to be blessed immediately. Would you break a tradition that has spanned centuries for petty gossip?"

"Gossip? You—" he looked over Silvano's shoulder and lowered his voice, perhaps unwilling to incite a riot. "You murdered the Miestryri. This is unprecedented."

"I was defending myself, priest. And you'd do well to remember it."

The priest puffed out his chest and raised his chin. "This matter needs further investigation. Do not presume to force our hand. It will go poorly for you." The priest's eyes darted to a point over Silvano's shoulder, and he could feel the weight of the crowd's gazes on his back.

He fought back a shiver. How quickly the crowd could sway, and a riot would not necessarily benefit him. With great reluctance, he nodded and stepped back so the priests could pass to the shore.

The priest's words echoed in his mind long after the crowd had dispersed. It didn't matter if the people supported him or not. Without the priests' backing, his rule was doomed before it started. He needed to win them over, and fast.

2

After the funeral, Silvano wandered toward the docks where the smaller pleasure yachts and fishing boats bobbed in the water. The water here was too shallow for the naval fleet, which was kept elsewhere. Soft sand squished beneath his bare feet, and the waves washed in, licking at his toes before retreating back into the sea. The constant push and pull of the tides echoed within him. What he wanted to do and what was best for his country warred in his mind. His eyes rose to the cliffs where the water raged against the rocks, pummeling everything in its path with a savage brutality.

If he couldn't gain control of his throne, would that be his fate as well?

Silvano held a hand to the side, absentmindedly pulling at the waves, allowing the seawater to hover for a moment before dropping it back down again. With a violent sweep of his arm, he shoved the water back and sat on the now-dry patch of sand, resting his head on his knees. What was he going to do now? The priests had turned against him. Half of the guards and castle staff had deserted before his father's body was even cold. The rest stayed out of fear.

Had the Seer been wrong?

He peeked back the way he'd come. Jax followed at a distance, respectful of Silvano's need to be alone after the disastrous funeral. He hadn't pushed Silvano for details of his exile, even though it was obvious that he burned with curiosity. The guard trusted him implicitly. If only the rest of the people could do the same. Still, maybe it was time for him to be honest and share his story, at least with his most trusted guards and advisors.

A shriek pierced the silence, followed by a giggle and a loud splash. Silvano's head snapped up, and his eyes roved the water before catching sight of movement by the docks. Frowning, he pushed himself to his feet and moved closer to investigate.

"Glass, stop that! No, no. Not that one! Go get another pink one!" a child's voice squealed.

"Lucinda?" he called out, jogging closer. His nine-year-old sister treaded water just past the shallows. Seaweed hung from her tight, black curls, and water droplets beaded on her bronze skin. A mound of sea glass, coins, and shells were stacked on the edge of the dock. A small, gray dolphin nudged her shoulder with his nose.

Her green eyes widened when she caught sight of him, and her mouth stretched into a wide smile. "Sil! Come on in, the water's great. I'll even tell Glass not to nip at you this time."

"I'm afraid I'll have to decline your invitation." Silvano eyed the dolphin—her familiar—warily as it swam in circles around Lucinda. His hand went to his thigh where Glass had bitten him two years ago. Foul beast.

"Come on, please?" She pouted and batted her eyelashes. "I'll show you the underwater cavern I found. And there's a mama whale who's due to give birth any day now. She promised that I could name her calf."

"That sounds lovely, but..." His eyes scanned the beach. Other than Jax, it was deserted. Who had allowed her to go to the beach alone? "Lucy... you know better than to come down here by yourself. It's not safe."

"Because father's dead?" she asked, not even flinching. But then again, she'd always been the strongest of them all. Silvano's mother had died after giving birth to Arianna, and his father hadn't wasted time remarrying. When Lucinda came along a few years later, it was as though an old crone had been born inside the unusually silent newborn. She saw more than she spoke, and she seemed to spend her days in fantasy.

Silvano shook off his discomfort and crouched on the edge of the dock. "Because the country is destabilized. It's not fair, but someone might take advantage of that fact and use you against me. You'd be safe at the castle."

Her face puckered. "But Glass is down here. I can't…"

"I know." He sighed. Lucinda was a Squama, and like Brutums and Avems, she couldn't be separated from her familiar for long periods of time without feeling like her soul was being torn in two. Still, it was better to feel temporary pain than to be dead. He raised a palm and commanded the sea, lifting a wave beneath Lucy and depositing her on the dock, dripping wet. "You shouldn't be out here unprotected."

"I'm not unprotected." She scowled and jabbed a finger at him. "You're here."

"Not for much longer. I have responsibilities, just like you. Your tutors are probably beside themselves with worry, and you don't want to miss more of your lessons."

Lucy made a face. "They can't teach me anything I don't already know."

"Oh really? Can you calculate the distance between East Rock and Orgate? Can you speak all seven languages with as much fluency as our own? Do you know the proper etiquette for greeting the Magnate of Aravell without starting a war?"

"Why would I need to know all that? It's not like I'll ever leave Crystalmoor." She gestured toward the sea. "This is my home."

"Oh?" he teased. "Are you planning on growing gills and fins and spending the rest of your life in the water?"

Her eyebrows formed a vee and she tilted her head as if she were considering his words seriously. "Is that possible?"

"If only." Silvano sighed. He looked out beyond the horizon, imagining the possibilities. "We could swim away from this mess and start over, just the two of us. We could discover a new island, full of mangoes and coconuts and no rules."

"Oh, there would be rules—I would make them. I'd be queen with a crown of seaweed and shells, and you'd be my advisor."

"Just so." His lips quirked up into a genuine smile, and he tapped her on the nose. If only their lives could be so simple.

Lucy puffed herself up to her full height and her voice dropped an octave lower as she tried to be regal. "And as queen, my first decree is this; lobsters will no longer be on the menu."

"Lobsters? Really?"

"Yes. I met a grandfather lobster who claims to be four hundred years old."

Silvano choked back a laugh at her serious expression. "Lobsters can count?"

She put her hands on her hips and glared at him. "What is harder to believe, that a lobster can count or a lobster can lie?"

"That's a fair point."

"Exactly. It seems cruel to eat something that smart."

"If lobsters are so intelligent, don't you think chickens, cows, and pigs have a similar mental capacity?"

"Maybe." She shrugged. "But I can't speak to *them*."

"Well then, I suppose you're correct." Without warning, he leapt toward her, wrapping his arms around her middle. She squealed as he threw her back into the sea. A moment later, she burst from the surface, her hair plastered to her face. Long strands of curled seaweed crowned her head. Silvano sank into a mocking bow. "All hail Queen Lucinda, protector of crustaceans."

She giggled and picked the seaweed from her hair. He ducked as she threw it at him, but it still managed to hit him on the shoulder. "I changed my mind. The first rule is now 'No irritating brothers allowed on my island'," she said as she waded out of the surf.

Silvano walked to the end of the dock and stepped onto the sand. He offered her the crook of his arm. "Come on then, let's get you back to your tutors."

Lucy reached for his hand but hesitated before her fingertips could brush his palm. She clamped her lip between her teeth.

His stomach sank. "What is it?"

"Sil… I heard what the people are calling you. Is it true?"

Silvano stiffened, fighting to keep his expression neutral. "It doesn't matter what they call me. What do you believe?"

"I don't know what to believe anymore."

He swallowed the lump in his throat. "No matter what, I hope you know that I would never harm you or our sister. I… I need you to trust me. To believe me when I tell you this. The two of you are the only family I have left, and we need to stick together."

She trotted over, her feet leaving footprints on the wet sand, and wrapped her small arms around his waist. "Okay, Sil. I trust you."

He pressed a kiss to the crown of her head, blinking away the burning in his eyes. "I won't let anything happen to you. I promise."

A wave of protectiveness flowed through him. He would protect her, would keep her safe in the coming months, no matter what happened.

But those hurt worst by conflict were rarely the ones directly involved.

3

Hours after he had delivered a squawking Lucinda into the capable arms of her tutors, Silvano found himself seated in the council room, suffering through his small council's discussion on the most insipid subjects known to mankind. His eyes glazed over as the minister of sanitation highlighted the advantages of building an underground sewer system beneath the city, and the logistics of installing indoor plumbing in every house. By the time the council started haggling over the benefits of copper versus lead pipes, Silvano had abandoned all pretense of listening.

Jax paced inside the door, throwing questioning glances his way every twenty seconds. Silvano had managed to ignore them so far, but his patience was wearing thin. To make things worse, one of the servants had built up an impressive yet unnecessary fire in the stone fireplace. Unfortunately, it made the room stifling, and he wasn't sure if the sweat running down his face was as a result of the heat, or his growing guilt.

He still hadn't opened up to his guards or advisors about his exile or the circumstances of his Gifting. He wanted their approval and support more than anything, but for some reason, he'd held his tongue. Which was ridiculous, when he thought about it. Having a Gift should make him more qualified to be Miestryri, in theory, but he was afraid that they would abandon him if they learned the truth. Perhaps they would say that the Magi had left him a dreg for a reason, and he was playing with the natural order by being Gifted later in life.

If only they knew the truth—that the Order had been selectively Gifting people for hundreds of years for no reason other than an obscure prophecy. But people had believed their lies for so long that the truth would seem false.

Sweeping away the pile of correspondences heaped on the table, Silvano lifted his head to stare at Jax. Between approving a dozen permits to build new homes and shops, and filtering through hundreds of citizen complaints, he was beginning to realize how tedious running a kingdom could be. No wonder he'd escaped as frequently as possible in his adolescence. Why would anyone willingly subject themselves to the horrors of paperwork when they could literally be doing anything else instead? Sweat dripped into his eye, and he wiped a palm across his face to ease the sting.

The newly appointed naval officer leaned forward in his chair and slid a stack of papers across the table. Silvano eyed him appraisingly, comparing him to his father's veteran officer, currently rotting in the dungeon next to Lucan. He seemed too young for the position, and too in love with his freshly grown mustache which he twisted as frequently as possible. He'd have to move quickly to secure the respect of his men, otherwise they'd eat him alive. "Sire, this is my official request for a dozen new ships."

Silvano raised his eyebrows. "I wasn't aware that we were at war."

"Well," the naval officer shifted in his chair and pulled at the collar of his uniform, "We're technically not yet, but it doesn't hurt to be prepared. With the Rei invading Lingate, it's only a matter of time before he sets his sights east. These ships could very well be the difference between victory and defeat."

"I see." Silvano twisted to look at the treasurer —a woman who looked like she was moments away from a nap or death. It wasn't entirely clear. She'd been the treasurer when his grandfather was still in diapers, and with each passing year, her hairline receded further. "Can we afford to fund the construction?"

"If we impose higher taxes, yes," she said in a frail voice. "You could begin construction within a month."

"At what cost?" The minister of the people protested. He half rose out of his seat, palms plastered to the table. His chest heaved with indignation, and spittle pelted everyone unfortunate enough to be seated nearby. "Sire, I beg you to see this madness for what it is. If you impose additional taxes, you will see riots in the streets. The people are suffering enough! Why should they pay a single coin more for glorified pleasure yachts?"

"Pleasure yachts?" The naval officer slammed a fist to the table. "Each vessel is equipped with two dozen crossbows and harpoons!"

"Can the people feed their children with crossbow bolts? We haven't had a war at sea in over a century!"

"Belosian pirates—"

"Those godless heathens slinging pig dung are hardly a formidable naval fleet. A half-trained child is strong enough alone to capsize their boats. This request is unreasonable."

"Enough!" Silvano pressed his palms to his temples and took a deep breath. "It might come as a surprise that Kearar, being a desert nation, does not have a naval fleet. If they were to attack, it would be from land. Furthermore, Rei Tomar and I are childhood friends," he said, completely glossing over the fact that Tomar had captured him during his last visit to the Mubali Oasis with the intention of selling him back to his father. After all, what friendship didn't have petty squabbles and misunderstandings? He shook his head. "I will not take food from children to fund shiny new toys for the navy!"

"But, sir—"

"No, my word on this is final. You're dismissed. We'll reconvene in a week's time to discuss the rest." No one moved. The council exchanged loaded looks, causing Silvano's temper to flare. "Was I unclear?"

"Forgive us, sire, but there's one last issue on our docket for today." The minister of the people shot a pointed look at Silvano's unblemished forehead. "While we appreciate that you took time from your busy schedule to arrange this meeting, you haven't been anointed Miestryri yet. Until you are, you simply don't have the authority to—"

"Rest assured that the matter is being handled promptly. Once I am Miestryri in an official capacity, your loyalty will be rewarded. I don't think I need to express how I would reward disloyalty," he said, allowing the unspoken threat to hang in the air. He sat back in his seat as the council gathered their papers and filed out the door. It might not have won him any favors, but they needed to be reminded of who was in charge during these crucial decisions. He had faith that the council would be working smoothly within a month's time. Jax stopped pacing, crossed his arms, and fixed Silvano with a hard stare. "Yes?"

"Look, I don't want you to think that I'm questioning you or doubting you in any way. You will always be my Miestryri, no matter what happens." He resumed his infernal pacing, wringing his hands together. "But when things happen that I can't explain, then I start wondering what you're trying to hide…"

"Jax, for the love of the sea god, stop rambling and just spit out what's bothering you."

Jax nodded and pulled a chair out from the table to sit down. He leaned forward and rested his elbows on his knees. "I saw you manipulate water, both at the funeral and at the docks, and I wasn't the only one. Your step-mother is spreading rumors among the elite and sowing discord amongst your supporters. They think it's some kind of trick. I held my tongue this long, but I think we deserve some answers. When you were exiled, you left as a dreg. Now, somehow, you return as an Irrigo. How… how is this possible?"

"It's a long story," Silvano said, releasing a shaking breath. "Honestly, I don't know where to start."

"The beginning seems appropriate. What happened when you were exiled?"

"Mikkal and I crossed into the southern border of Lingate. He wished to be discreet and stick to the wilds, but I was stubborn and insisted that no one would dare harm a prince, even if he was a dreg. Mikkal seemed distant at the time. I thought he was upset with me or the situation itself—what Shield would be delighted to train for a decade only to serve a disgraced prince? I had no idea that he was struggling with his morality instead. Unbeknownst to me, my father had approached Mikkal the night before we left and paid him to assassinate me. We traveled for a week until we reached the southern outpost of Canaich where the Rudven clan had settled to gather strength. I insisted on lodging in an inn and purchasing a hot meal for the two of us.

"It was one foolish decision in a long line of foolish decisions. It doesn't matter where you go in Lingate, the strong rule and the weak are prey. And for them? All dregs are prey, regardless of their birth. I still don't understand how they found us. Maybe they had a Veniet, or maybe Father had sent out wanted posters, but we were cornered…"

The inn had seen better days. It had probably been a welcoming beacon to weary travelers in its heyday, or at least it had once possessed a functioning door. I walked up to the gaping hole in the wall and peered inside. For someone who had grown accustomed to the refined behavior of the upper echelons of society, Lingate can be quite a shock. The patrons were dragging no fewer than three dead bodies from the room while the apparent victors were throwing back one celebratory drink after another. There was no way we'd blend in, not with me wearing my best silk doublet and crimson cloak. That suited me just fine. I had no intention of being overlooked like some commoner.

Mikkal took one look at the inn and turned around, probably debating if he should simply tie me up and haul my spoiled behind to the nearest cave to hide.

"Mikkal, unless you wish to snap the hilt of your sword off entirely, I suggest you relax." My smile widened as his scowl deepened.

He shot me a look as if to say, 'Unless you want to be a corpse, I suggest you follow my lead.' It can be a tricky thing to communicate with someone who doesn't speak, but after being around my Shield for a decade, I find that he's more expressive than most people if you know how to read him. I pushed past him into the room and flashed my coin purse to the nearest worker—who needs strength when you could buy it? In retrospect, I'm surprised Mikkal didn't run me through right there and save himself the trouble.

The barmaid told us to have a seat anywhere we liked, and she'd bring out some cottage stew. I eyed the central table with longing, but Mikkal grabbed my arm and dragged me to a dark corner booth, shoving me in as far as I would go before sitting on the edge of the bench. He left his sword in its sheath, but he drew a dagger and laid it on the bench next to him—a warning for anyone who might cause us trouble.

I scoffed at his paranoia.

As promised, the barmaid soon brought over two troughs of stew, two pints of ale and a loaf of dark, seeded bread. I had just lifted a spoonful of the slop to my lips when a rough-looking man with arms larger than my thighs stomped over to our booth. I assume he had at one point owned a mouth full of teeth, but some were conspicuously missing now, and the ones that remained were stained a deep yellow. And the smell... phew. If I had eaten anything at that point, it would have promptly made a reappearance.

I covered my nose with my hand and said, "Good evening, sir. Can we help you with something?"

Without a word, he swept an arm across the table, sending our food flying. Hot stew splattered over my clothes. "No dregs allowed," he said in that gravely, savage accent of Lingate.

Mikkal jumped from his seat, drawing his sword in one fluid motion, keeping me hidden. The man pulled an axe from the strap on his back and swung it in a brutal arc toward his throat. Mikkal blocked the blow and pushed him backward into a table, sending tankards flying. The man roared and charged again. More patrons crowded near, eager to see the action, and two more joined the fight against us.

Well, not us, per se. Mikkal. I was useless. Up until that point, I'd shown no interest in swordplay, and the swordmaster at East Rock swore that I would be skewered by the time I hit adulthood. He was wrong, thankfully, but his opinion on my skills was painfully accurate. What use was learning to fight when I had a legendary Shield to guard my back? Leaving Mikkal to handle the ruffians, I did what I do best—save my own skin. I slipped out of the booth and through the kitchens past the gaping Pistor who clutched a meat cleaver in his shaking hands. I had just stepped outside when rough hands grabbed my stew-splattered doublet and slammed me against the wall. A blade pricked my neck and I froze.

"*Don't move or I'll cut ya.*"

I held my breath and lowered my eyes to look at my attacker. She barely came up to my chest in height, but I'd never seen a more terrifying creature. Her face and arms were riddled with deep scars, and the top of her ear had been cut off. Her tunic was dirty and full of holes. But the real terror was in her eyes—desperation. It was clear that she was a survivor. Someone who had experienced true suffering, and now she had nothing to lose. She was like a scavenger, letting the sharks fight over a meal then darting in for the kill while they were distracted. With Mikkal fighting the thugs inside, I was in very real trouble.

I swallowed and plastered a tight smile on my face. I was Crown Prince Silvano Miore', I could charm my way out of any situation, no matter how unpleasant. "My lady, perhaps there's something I can do to assist you? If you're in need of a hot meal and lodging, it appears as though a few rooms have been recently vacated."

A loud crash followed by shouts from inside the inn punctuated my claim. I dared a glance at the door, but there was no sign of my Shield anywhere. What was taking so long? Was he fighting everyone one at a time?

"Shut up with yer fancy words." She ran a hand down my side, and I felt the strings of my coin purse loosen.

"If I might be so bold, there's no need to rob me when I'm more than willing to assist you."

"Welcome to Lingate, love. If ye're not the hunter, ye're the prey." She juggled the coin purse in her hand, a satisfied grin blossoming on her face at the weight. Then her face hardened, and she dug the tip of her dirk into my neck. *"Don't bother following me. If I see ya again, I'll kill ya."*

And with that, she backed away and ran off into the darkness.

I stared after her, the beginnings of desire forming. Oh, not romantic. Not by any stretch of the imagination. She was fierce, brutal, and dangerous. Surviving my exile was proving more challenging than I'd anticipated, and I wanted that demon woman on my side.

Silvano trailed off at the memory. Mikkal had tracked the woman to a small lean-to a few days south of Canaich but she hadn't been alone. It turned out that she was protecting a tiny slip of a girl named Tova, and she was more than willing to kill to keep her safe. After some tense negotiations and even more death threats, the woman, Wynn, had agreed to team up with us. Their odds of survival increased with numbers. "We spent the next year on the run, watching each other's backs. I knew that one day, I wanted to return home. I wanted to reclaim my position as heir. But first, I needed to learn more about the Order and why some people are Gifted while others are cursed to be dregs. I heard about a library in the ancient ruins of an old castle in southern Esterwyn, and we decided to investigate. On our way there, we ran into two fellow travelers. The woman, Mara, claimed that she'd been a dreg her whole life, but the power in her spoke of a different story. Now, I needed to know more. If it were possible for her to develop a Gift, I wanted one, too. For the first time, I felt hope."

"That's a lovely story," Jax said, gesturing to Silvano, "but it doesn't explain how you were Gifted."

"I'm getting to that. Our journey led us to the frozen wasteland of Tregydar where we found a settlement completely removed from the influence of the Order. It was there that we met a Seer—"

"A what?"

"A Seer. It's like a… female Magi. She can see the future. Opal, the Seer, gave us a place to stay and taught us of the treachery of the Order. It was because of her that I was not only given my Gift, but also a safe place to train."

Jax's brow furrowed. "And what happened to the others?"

"Mara was captured by the Order. In truth, I had hoped that she would join my cause in reclaiming my throne, but it was not to be. She's probably still a captive. I'm ashamed to say it, but I hope she is. It's for the best. A power like hers is too dangerous to let go free." He squeezed his eyes shut as the memory of their botched attack flooded through his mind. "A few weeks later, Opal had a vision that the Order was going to invade Tregydar and wipe out the settlement. She evacuated their home and sent Wynn and me in two different ways. She told me it was time to reclaim my birthright. That in two months' time, I should go to the Warlord and ask for help. Then I should come here and take my place as the crown prince. Obviously, I decided to cut out the middle man and come here directly. It seemed more efficient at the time."

"I'm still struggling with the idea that dregs can be Gifted. I never thought it was possible… It flies in the face of everything we've been taught."

"I was as shocked as you, but you can see the evidence here." Silvano stood and walked to the window that overlooked the city. Everyone depended on him to do the right thing, but change came with a cost. For Crystalmoor, the price would be their ignorance. "When I am Miestryri, I will stop at nothing to rid our country of the Order's corruption. As Opal once said, it's a rot that must be carved out and destroyed."

"You're already up against a fair amount of opposition from the masses. If you attempt to drive out the Order altogether, you'll be facing an all-out rebellion."

"As Miestryri, it is my duty to do what's best for my people."

"I only hope that you will do the right thing."

"Do you doubt me?"

"Of course not, I—"

The door crashed open and two guards entered the room, dragging a bound prisoner behind them. The guards roughly shoved him to his knees before Silvano. The boy seemed young, no older than fourteen or fifteen. His blue eyes held a glimmer of defiance, rather than fear, and his pale skin was flushed.

"We apprehended him skulking around the treasury, sire," the guard said, giving the boy a kick with his boot.

"Was anything missing?"

"No. We've confirmed that everything is secure and accounted for."

"So, what should we do with you?" Silvano brushed the straw-colored hair back from the boy's face before tilting his chin up to get a better look at him. "Why did you come here? And how did you get in without someone stopping you?" He directed the pointed question to his guards who fidgeted under his scathing glare.

"If I may, sire, we don't believe he was working alone."

"I agree with your assessment. Anyone with the intellectual capabilities of a sea sponge would agree! How else would a child from the slums know his way around the castle so well? Have you searched him?"

"Yes, sire." The guard unfolded a piece of parchment and held it up. "It appears to be a map."

Silvano snatched it from his hand and almost dropped it. Not only was it a near perfect rendering of the castle layout, but the labels... he'd recognize that handwriting anywhere. What did *she* want so badly from the treasury that she was willing to send someone to get it?

Jax leaned closer to get a better look at the paper. No doubt he'd drawn the same conclusion when he whispered, "We should torture him for information."

Silvano wished he could have been surprised by the suggestion, but he'd be lying if he said he was. Torture was one of his father's favorite methods of getting someone to talk, but he didn't want to be like his father. He wanted to be better. He wanted his people's love, not their fear.

He looked at the boy again. He had the rough edges of someone who was used to struggling. He was just a little too thin, his clothes a little too torn. "What is your name?"

The boy spit in his face.

Jax pulled his hand back to hit the boy, who flinched violently to the side before the blow could even land. Silvano shouted, "Wait!"

Jax looked at him in confusion but obeyed and lowered his hand to his side. Silvano wouldn't boast that he was the best at reading people but growing up in the court of sycophants and backstabbers had its advantages. There was more to this boy than a simple thief. He recognized the look in his eyes as if he were looking in the mirror. He was a casualty of a system that didn't care who it hurt, so long as those who were in power stayed in power, no matter the cost. Jax protested as Silvano lowered himself to kneel before the boy.

Feeling a connection to him, Silvano reached out and placed an arm on the boy's shoulder. "You're a dreg."

His eyes bugged out of his head. "How did you—"

"It's obvious. You come from a poor family and were likely born in the slums. Your parents tried their best to protect you, but they couldn't stop the persecution. This made you feel powerless and angry. When the Miestryri died, you thought it would get worse. You didn't know me, so you turned to Arianna. Did she come to you with an offer? Did she offer you protection in exchange for your support?"

The boy gaped, his jaw working like he was trying to chew through a clam shell.

"I know what you're going through. I grew up a dreg, too, and I have experienced that prejudice firsthand. I want to make things better for everyone…" Silvano trailed off. "What is your name?"

"Bas."

Silvano smiled and nodded his head. "Bas, I can't improve your situation if Crystalmoor is divided. A war would make things worse for everyone. Now, I don't know what Arianna is planning, but I do know that she's probably making her decisions based on hearsay and false rumors. If we want to create a country where everyone is treated equally, regardless of station, we need to be united. You can help by giving us information." He held up the map. "I know she gave you this map, Bas. Where is my sister?"

The guarded mask slammed back onto Bas's face, and he looked away, unable to meet Silvano's gaze. "I can't tell you that."

"Can't, or won't?"

"Won't."

"I see. That's unfortunate," he said, trying to hide his disappointment. Now he began to realize why his father used torture to get information. Would it be so bad? If a bit of pain could help him find his sister, would it justify the situation? Just how many lives would be saved? If Arianna was moving against him, too many innocent people would get caught in the cross fire. He needed to speak with her to understand her motivations. So far, she had avoided causing harm to the populace, but who knew what she'd be willing to do to unseat him and secure her position. She was his sister and he loved her, but she was power-hungry and conniving. With more than a little regret, he stood and nodded to Jax. It was for the best.

Jax began to drag a struggling Bas from the room. Silvano closed his eyes and steeled himself against what was coming. It was necessary. Maybe if he told himself enough times, he would eventually believe it.

No.

This was wrong. "Stop!"

Every head in the room snapped to look at Silvano.

Before he changed his mind, Silvano said, "Release him."

Jax hurried to his side and lowered his voice into a whisper. "Sire, he has the information we need. Give us an hour and we'll find out where she's hidden and what her plans are. We could stop a war."

"Not like this. Release him. Now."

Jax gritted his teeth, but he nodded for a guard to cut Bas's bonds.

Shame flooded him, and suddenly he was the one unable to look the boy in the eyes. No information was worth that. "Escort him to the door and let him go."

"Yes, sire," Jax said, his voice filled with venom.

After he had left, Silvano motioned for one of the guards, a younger man with cow eyes and a dimpled chin, to approach. "Follow him at a distance. Make sure he doesn't know he's being followed, then report back immediately. I need to know numbers, how well they are armed, and where they are located. Then, we can plan."

4

The temple of the sea god perched at the top of the cliffs against an orange and red sky. In keeping with tradition, everything within the temple had been pulled from the water, from the sandstone altar to the preserved seaweed 'curtains' that fluttered in the breeze. The walls, made from driftwood branches woven together, looked eerily like leviathan bones—no doubt to inspire awe in the simple-minded who would rather cling to the old ways rather than embrace progress.

Silvano forced his feet to move forward. He'd rather be dunked in a tank of ravenous sharks than step foot in the temple, but he had no choice. If he wanted to keep the support of the small council, he needed to become Miestryri officially. He would somehow convince the high priest to anoint him.

"Would you like me to go in with you?" Jax rested a hand on his shoulder.

Silvano shrugged him off. "That won't be necessary. I hardly think that an elderly priest is a threat to my well-being."

"You know that's not what I meant. After what happened…"

"I can manage to hold a civil conversation with the man," he snapped.

Jax nodded and stepped back to stand with the other two guards who insisted on following him everywhere. While he didn't say anything out loud, Silvano could almost hear his unspoken words. *You'd better… You have a lot riding on this.* He knew that better than anyone. If he couldn't convince the priests to anoint him, then he might as well hand the country to Arianna and go back into exile.

He hesitated under the archway, his nose wrinkling at the strong fish odor emanating from the whale oil lamps. The last time he'd been to the temple was when his mother had bled to death on her birthing bed. He'd begged the god to spare her life and had received nothing but silence and grief in return. Nothing had changed since that day. A basin of sea salt waited by the entrance. A spiraling sea glass mosaic spanned the floor. In the center of the room on a pedestal was a massive oyster shell fountain, large enough for a man to bathe in. Silvano stepped forward and ran his hands across the surface of the water. A handful of coins, gems, and sea glass rested in the bottom of the fountain, waiting to be fished out by the priests.

If his mother had survived, would things be different? He closed his eyes, remembering one of his last happy memories of her.

It was a hot summer night and not even the cool breeze blowing in the open windows could bring relief from the tormenting heat. Mama chuckled as I kicked off the sheets and sprawled out on the bed. She tried cuddling next to me, but I shoved her away, not wanting to feel her sticky skin on mine. We'd spent the whole day on the beach, playing in the waves, and trying to catch a mermaid. I didn't have the heart to tell her that I'd stopped believing in mermaids a year ago.

'You're going to spoil him with fantasy,' his father had said. 'He's six now, and it's time he puts away this childish nonsense.' His mother had assured his father that she would take his wishes into account and, as usual, done as she'd pleased anyway.

She propped her head on a pillow, her long, brown hair sprawling everywhere, and smiled softly at me. I smiled back, letting my tired eyes drink her in. I'd never seen anyone more beautiful. She was a goddess. Her pearl-white complexion was a star in the night sky next to my father's midnight skin, and her pale blue eyes sparkled with love and mischief.

"Oh, my little cuttlefish. How I love you."

"I love you too, Mama." I scooted closer, but not too close, and she pressed a kiss to my forehead.

"There's something I need to tell you." She reached out and took my hand in hers. "You're going to have a little brother or sister by winter's start."

I didn't know much about babies, but this sounded like a terrible idea. Jax's mama just had a baby—a pink, wrinkly, squalling thing—and all she did was eat, cry, and sleep. Forgetting about how it was too hot to snuggle, I wiggled my way into her arms and buried my face in her shoulder. "Can't you stop it?"

She laughed, the soft musical sound filling the room. "No, my sweet boy."

"But won't this mean you can't love me as much?"

"Impossible. Don't you know that love can only grow? I love you so much already, and once the baby is born, there will be enough to fill up the sea until it overflows." She sounded so sincere that I had to believe her. Then she sighed and cupped my chin in her hand. "You look so much like your father."

"Mama, will you sing my song for me?"

She nodded and opened her mouth and sang:

Goodbye, fair prince, I'll see you again,

I will come back, though I do not know when.
I'm leaving tomorrow on waters of gold,
Beyond the horizon lie riches untold.

Goodbye, sweet prince, I'm never too far,
I'll find my way home by the light of our star.
Adventure and fortune are calling for me,
Over the waves to the edge of the sea.

Goodbye, dear prince, I'll see you soon,
Beneath the smile of a midsummer moon.
Look to the east and keep watch for my sail,
We'll sip blackberry wine as I tell you the tale.

Goodbye, brave prince, please do not fear,
The end of my journey is soon drawing near.
Death's bitter kiss can't keep us apart,
And you, my love, are dear to my heart.

"This is a sight I never imagined I'd see again. The exiled prince has finally come to worship at the altar of the sea god." The priest's reedy voice was barely a whisper sending icy shivers across his neck, yet Silvano would recognize it anywhere as it pulled him from his memory. And like a plate of raw salted seaweed, slimy to the tongue, it was equally as repulsive.

Silvano quickly wiped the wetness from his eyes, keeping his face turned away. "Would strangling the sea god's high priest in his own temple count as worship?" Anger coursed through his veins, and his hands clenched on the rim on the oyster shell. He forced himself to take a deep breath. As much as he despised the situation, he would have to cater to the priest's whims. Until Silvano was anointed, the priest held all the power. "Apologies."

"We all serve him in our own ways, and for some, faith does not come easily. The question is why you feel such an extreme act necessary."

"The sea god and I have a bit of a tumultuous history. If you don't mind, I'd prefer to keep this brief."

"But of course. So why are you here?"

Silvano turned to face the treacherous priest who had long since removed the ceremonial robe, replacing it with a basic white shift. A single strand of shells wrapped around his waist and fell to the floor where it clattered around his bare toes. The light from the lanterns set his hair alight, giving the priest an otherworldly glow that Silvano found disconcerting. He swallowed, refusing to show his discomfort. "You embarrassed me in front of my people."

A small smile played on the priest's lips, as though Silvano were still a child instead of a man in his own right. "You embarrassed yourself."

"Every Miestryri is anointed as his predecessor crests the horizon into his next life. It's a tradition that spans the centuries, and you threw that in my face by calling doubt on my claim. You will rectify this slight at once."

"The path of succession is… unclear at the moment."

"It was my right—"

"Your right?" He folded his hands at his waist and spoke slowly. "You come into this holy place like a petulant child whose toy has been taken away. You show none of the patience or wisdom necessary for the honor. So what, pray tell, gives you the right to be Miestryri?"

"I am the firstborn of the former Miestryri."

"The same Miestryri that you killed, correct?" The priest lifted in hand in a placating gesture. "No need to get defensive. I have no authority over such things, and I'd rather spare you from spewing excuses that we both know won't matter. You've created a stain on your soul that not even salt and sand can scrub away."

"I'm hardly the first."

"No, and I doubt you'll be the last. Perhaps during your exile, you spent too much time around those who not only view patricide and regicide as legitimate pathways to succession, they actively encourage them. But you're not in Kearar or Lingate right now, and you're a fool if you believe the people of Crystalmoor will forgive you so easily. Why should I anoint you?"

"If my birth won't sway you, then maybe my Gift will." Silvano pulled his shoulders back and stood to his full height to glare down at the weak-backed priest. He would not be cowed. Not when he was this close to gaining everything he wanted. "I am a powerful Irrigo—perhaps the most powerful in over one hundred years. Surely you can see that it is my destiny. The sea chose me for a reason, and I will rule my people."

"Rule?" The priest cocked his head to the side. "Not serve?"

Silvano winced and hurried to cover his mistake. As much as he hated to admit it, he needed the priests. No one would follow a Miestryri who hadn't been anointed. "Ah, I misspoke. Obviously, I meant serve, as generations of Miestryri have done for thousands of years. Crystalmoor will thrive under my care, you can be assured of that."

"The strength of your Gift, your power, does not guarantee that the sea has chosen you. Your own uncle was the firstborn in his family, and his ability to manipulate water was legendary. Greater than yours, I would wager, if such things were allowed for us priests. Though it was blasphemous, the lowborn whispered that he was the reincarnation of the sea god himself. But when it came time to choose succession, the sea passed him over in favor of your father."

"Why?" Silvano couldn't stop the question before it escaped his lips. He had never met his uncle, who had left the palace before he was born. Rumor had it that the man had fled in the middle of the night with a schooner and a skeleton crew, never to be seen again. Silvano hadn't realized that his uncle, not his father, had been the firstborn.

"Why are some blessed with long, healthy lives while children fall ill and die, beyond the help of our Healers? Why do some set sail in a storm and return triumphant while others disappear in fair weather, never to be seen again. Surely, our fragile brains cannot comprehend the greater mysteries. We must accept that the oldest and most powerful are not necessarily the best choice for the throne."

"You will not help me then," Silvano said, his shoulders sagging.

"We must wait and watch for a sign. I suggest you meditate on this in quiet reflection. The sea god will better hear your pleas if you first make an offering." The priest gestured to the fountain, his meaning clear. He would be happy to anoint Silvano... for the right price.

"Will he?" Silvano asked in a biting voice, unable to mask the hatred from his tone. "And how many widows have you told that very thing as they were praying for their husbands return? How many children as they beg for their mothers while they bleed out? How much have you profited from their hopes and their grief?"

The priest's face filled with pity. "We have all experienced loss, and it grows no easier as time passes. It is difficult to accept, but if the sea god wants to claim someone for his own, there is nothing we mortals can do to stop it. You can stop death no easier than you can stop the waves from crashing on the shore."

"Let me be clear, priest. I have no interest in stopping death. My plans are for the living, and I cannot help them without this power. You will anoint me as Miestryri, or I will find someone who will. I doubt all your priests are as *pious* as you." Silvano let the threat hang heavy between them.

The priest's lips pulled back from his teeth, and Silvano took a step backward. "You can sit up on your throne and play king as much as you wish, but it changes nothing. Chosen or not, the sea god cannot reach those hidden behind stone walls, so far from the sea."

Silvano rushed out of the temple before the priest could see how much his words had shaken him. He blew past an overly-inquisitive Jax and didn't stop until he came to the fork in the path. If he turned right, it would lead him back to the castle where he could shutter himself in his rooms and refuse to speak with anyone. But that wouldn't solve his problem. As tempting as it was, he couldn't ignore the situation, hoping it would fix itself. Reluctantly, he chose the left path.

There was one person he needed to see. If anyone could help him make sense of this mess, it was Olielle.

5

"Don't fret, my friend. The sea gods haven't claimed me yet, and they won't get me tonight, either." I shoved Mikkal to the side and hurried to Olielle's house. The overly-clingy Shield had only gotten worse since the assassination attempt, and if he didn't give me some space, I was going to explode. I ran a hand down my finest silk doublet and adjusted my cloak before knocking on the door. This was the last night I had to keep up this charade, and I was determined to sell it properly.

Olielle answered the door a moment later. The way her face lit up at the sight of me made me question just how fake our engagement was to her. She pressed a kiss to each of my cheeks, and I stepped back to hold her at arm's length. "Olielle, you look positively ravishing!"

She tucked a strand of long, auburn hair behind her ear while tilting her head toward Mikkal. "Won't you come in, my lord?"

"With pleasure." Once I got rid of my Shield, at least. I turned to Mikkal and said, "I'll be back at dawn, then we'll embark on a glorious adventure!"

He shook his head defiantly, making no move to leave. I could feel Olielle fidgeting behind me, and my nerves began to grate. "Let me remind you that Lucan tried to assassinate my father, not me. Furthermore, I highly doubt that my betrothed has any nefarious designs on my life. I am perfectly safe here. Now, leave me. Go and visit your sister if you must have something with which to occupy your time. That is a command."

Without waiting for him to obey, I grabbed Olielle by the arm and hurried inside, slamming the door behind us, making her giggle. She waited a minute before peeking out the window, and her entire body relaxed. "He's leaving."

"It's about time!" I said, throwing myself down onto the sofa. "Do you know how exhausting it is to be followed every minute of every day?"

"And how do you think he feels?"

I twisted in my seat to watch her walk into the kitchen. She returned a moment later with a bottle of vintage red and two long-stemmed glasses. "What is that supposed to mean?"

Her full lips quirked into a smile as she popped the cork and poured the wine before offering me a glass. "It must be torture to deal with you constantly. Between your flaunting authority and rampant partying, I'm surprised he hasn't killed you already."

"How positively vicious! I'm wounded!" I took the glass and gave it a suspicious sniff. "Unless you're planning on poisoning me yourself. I'm fairly certain that depriving the world of my devilishly good looks is tantamount to treason."

"Yes, that would be the real crime for sure," she said dryly. Then her face softened, and she sat next to me on the sofa. "Are you okay?"

"I'm fine. Personally, I think my father is overreacting a bit, but exile just might be the best thing to happen to me. Now, I'll have the opportunity to do some digging on the Order. I might even make alliances for when I return. My father will have to see that I'm the best choice to be named successor."

"I hope you're right. We've worked too hard to secure your position to lose it now."

"And your position? We both know you are the true mastermind here."

"Obviously. Without my help, Arianna would have destroyed you by now. Better to be viewed as incompetent and underestimated by your opponents than seen as a threat" She clinked her glass against mine

before taking a small sip. "I've put together a bag for you. In it you'll find maps, coin, lists of safe places, and enough food to see you through to Lingate. Don't worry about Crystalmoor. I'll make sure to maintain your presence here until it's safe to come home."

I leaned forward to kiss her on the cheek. "You are too thoughtful. I don't deserve you."

"No, you don't."

***

More than a year had passed since that night—the night before his exile. He had sent Mikkal away as he visited Olielle at her father's house, so wrapped up in his plans that he had missed his Lucan's scheming. How young and foolish he had been. But that was a different house, and he was a different man.

Waving to his guards to stay back, Silvano walked up the sea glass-crusted walkway, framed with metal poles and hanging lanterns on either side. While the lawn had been meticulously manicured, the flower beds held only a handful of tropical plants and shrubs, spaced evenly apart. He hummed in appreciation at the mansion, taking in the white polished brick, sloping overhangs, and recessed windows. It reeked of new construction, modeled after the modern, clean architecture of

Aravell, and it was only a matter of time before the rest of the upper class ordered renovations for their homes.

Olielle had always been a trend setter, but this stark monstrosity felt nothing like the warmth he remembered. She had filled every inch of her father's home with treasures they'd find at the beach in memory of her mother who had passed away a decade ago. Her light had dimmed, like a cloud passing in front of the sun, but it had not vanished.

Had his exile been the catalyst for her transformation?

Before he lost his nerve, Silvano rapped on the door. He took a step back and wiped a gloved finger over the nearest window, frowning when it came away clean. They hadn't washed them in seawater for luck? As much as he despised the old way's superstitions, this was one that not even he would skip. Did they want to lose their home when the next hurricane passed through?

The door cracked open. An imposing man with ebony skin, a few inches taller than Silvano, filled the doorway. The short, black twists of his hair stuck up like spikes, and he glared down at Silvano with barely-concealed disdain. "You."

"How positively eloquent! I can see why Olielle likes you."

The man frowned, as if trying to decide if that had been a compliment or not. Before he burst a blood vessel from thinking too hard, Silvano sighed and said, "I need to speak with your wife."

"She doesn't—"

"Wonderful!" Silvano pushed past him and into the foyer of the mansion. Once inside, it was obvious that Olielle had been in charge of the interior decorating—everything was purple, from a soft lilac to a deep indigo. Thick rugs covered the hardwood floors. A mirror, framed with seashells, hung on the wall. Down the hallway, he caught a glimpse of cushioned settees, draped with plush pillows and blankets. Overall, the impression was a strange mix of wealth and comfort, and it was a relief to know that she hadn't lost herself completely.

The rich smell of seafood chowder and fresh-baked bread filled the space, making his mouth water. At the clanking of a spoon hitting a pot, Silvano turned his head toward the kitchen. "She truly is a fantastic cook, though I'm sure you already knew that. Has she made you her famous saltwater taffy yet? She and her mother would make a huge batch every year, pulling dozens of pounds over that rusty old hook. Does she still have it, by chance?"

The man gave a curt shake of his head. Hm... not the most gregarious fellow then. Such a pity. Olielle had always enjoyed stimulating conversations.

"Ah, such a shame. It was something of an heirloom in her family, though nothing could take those memories away from me. I never understood why they made it at the height of summer when the house was already scorching. Combined with the boiling ingredients and hours of pulling, it's no wonder her father threw me out of the house before they started shedding their layers." Silvano waggled his eyebrows suggestively. "But I always got the first taste when the other children came knocking."

Beside him, Olielle's husband bristled, perhaps wondering if he would be executed for laying hands on the heir and throwing him outside. Probably. But then again, Silvano wouldn't do that to Olielle. He peeked out of the corner of his eye at the man, trying to get his measure. He had better treat her like the goddess she was or he'd... dear god, was his eye actually twitching?

"If you'd be so kind as to wait in the sitting room, I will go find her," he said through clenched teeth, each word sounding like he was crunching glass.

Silvano dipped his head and strode down the hallway, feeling slightly guilty about trying to bait the poor man. It was clear he had a jealous constitution and not enough humor to make up for it. How had Olielle ended up with such a bland shell of a man? He huffed, settling down onto the velvet settee and kicking his legs out before him, ankles crossed. Being here was stranger than he'd expected. He'd never entertained romantic notions about Olielle, despite them being betrothed from infancy. She had been a close friend and confidant, and had they gotten married, it would have been nothing more than a political alliance.

That didn't stop his heart from racing when she stepped into the room wearing a floor-length gown that was clearly inspired by the Kerani suvali. The pale blue fabric, the exact shade of a tranquil sky, popped against her deep, golden skin and auburn hair. While her dress was peaceful, her eyes were anything but. Twin storms rounded on him, and he swallowed.

Olielle stared at him a moment longer than was polite before lowering her eyes and dipping into a shallow curtsy. "Miestryri, to what do we own the pleasure?" she asked, tight-lipped.

"I'm not Miestryri yet." His brows creased. This was not how he'd expected her to react. "Am I not permitted to visit a dear friend?"

Her eyes darted to where her husband lurked in the doorway, and Silvano could almost taste her panic. So that's what she was worried about? In Crystalmoor, betrothal bonds could only be broken by death—some archaic nonsense about the woman belonging to the man, body and soul, as soon as the contract was signed. It was one of those outdated laws that his father had never bothered changing during his reign. By rights, Silvano could kill her new husband and claim her for himself. It hurt that she thought so little of him. "You know I would never do that to you."

"You killed your father," she said in a matter-of-fact voice.

He stared at her a long minute, debating whether or not to be honest. "I did."

A pause, then, "Was it intentional?"

"You should know be better than that by now, after everything we've been through."

"I knew the boy who left, but the man who returned is a stranger. I don't know what he's capable of."

Perhaps for the first time, Silvano was at a loss for words. What was he capable of? He closed his eyes, remembering the past year away from Crystalmoor. As difficult as it had been, he had grown up in that time. But underneath it all, he was still the same man. And now, he had a chance to make things better for his people. "I need your help."

Her eyebrows shot upward. "What can I do?" she asked, her voice skeptical. He couldn't blame her. In his twenty-six years, his greatest accomplishment thus far was swallowing a toxic, purple-spotted octopus without vomiting immediately—not exactly a stellar recommendation for his capacity to rule.

It was a question he'd expected, nevertheless. And if he could win her over, perhaps he would have a chance. Silvano gestured between them. "There's a reason why you and I were betrothed. You and your father were two of our biggest social influencers among the upper circles. As much as I would have liked to have been welcomed home with cheers and acclaim, that will clearly not happen. The priests are refusing to anoint me. Let's just say that my hold on Crystalmoor is tenuous, at best. If I'm to maintain my title and become Miestryri, I need the backing of the upper class more than ever." He told her about Arianna, the small council, and the priest's refusal to anoint him.

She nodded slowly and reached up to run a finger over her lower lip—a sure tell that she was absorbing his words. He could always count on her to gather the facts before making a decision. Even when playing tiles, she would take agonizing minutes before moving her piece. It was a trait that he once cursed, but now he valued. Olielle took a deep breath and rolled her eyes. "You're an idiot for not coming to me sooner."

Her husband gasped, but Silvano merely laughed. "That goes without saying. Do you see how dire my situation is?"

"You've had your share of trouble in the past, but this is…" Her eyes bulged, and she pressed a palm to her forehead. "What about Arianna?"

"I need her support as well." When Olielle protested, Silvano held up his hand. "No, it's true. Think about it beyond the nobility. She's beloved by the people. If she were to challenge me now, I don't think I would win."

Olielle released her breath and adopted a calculating look that he knew all too well. "And I suppose she hasn't shown her face yet?"

"Not even a glimpse since I returned. I don't like what it suggests."

"Neither do I. Either she believes the reports and is in hiding, or she is preparing her assault to challenge you." She clasped her hands behind her back and began to pace around the room, her face scrunched in concentration. "You'll need to move quickly to secure your place."

"How is that possible, considering the priests are refusing to anoint me?"

"They haven't outright refused though, correct?" When he mumbled an assent, she said, "You should be more… generous."

His eyebrows rose. He hadn't expected her to agree with bribing the priests. "You would have me give in to extortion?"

Olielle spun to face him, placing her hands on her hips. "Do you want my help or not?"

"Yes, but—"

"Then stop questioning my methods. If you want results, you need to show them you're willing to cooperate. Give a generous donation to the priests, and they will change their tune. And then there's your Gift. I've heard rumors that you're the strongest Irrigo alive."

"How does everyone seem to know my business this quickly? It's honestly ridiculous!"

"I assume you are being rhetorical, but the answer is spies, most likely. I'm sure your sister has several. If you want to win, you first need to know your enemy. So, is it true?"

"Well, I don't like to brag—" She let out a very unladylike snort and he said, "Fine. Yes, it's true. But the priest said that didn't matter. Did you know that my uncle was firstborn and a powerful Irrigo, too, yet the sea passed him over in favor of my father."

Olielle shot him a pointed look. "The sea passed him over? Or did your father make a sizeable donation to ensure the rule passed to him instead?"

"Fair point." The thought hadn't crossed his mind, but it would make sense.

"Now, you will still need to win over the people. Your father was heavy-handed with taxes which kept the lines between the upper and outer classes sharply defined. Arianna has been sowing good-will with the people for years, so you'll need to do some catching up here. I would recommend a six-month grace period in taxes for the poor."

"How am I supposed to bribe the priests without the revenue?"

"You haven't seen the treasury then. I would have assumed that was the first place you'd have gone after coming home."

"I have more important things on my mind than money."

"Clearly. Now, money is only one small portion of this, and it won't be enough in and of itself. The people will need to see a display of your power. You will show your skeptics that the sea chose you because of your might."

"You're suggesting I organize a demonstration."

"Exactly. You won't win everyone over, but it will make your sister question the wisdom in challenging you."

"I would need a large audience for this to be effective."

"The bigger the better in this case. As soon as your anointing is complete, you'll need to send out a mandate and gather everyone at the cliffs. Once they see what you can do, they won't be able to help themselves. They will support you."

Silvano clasped her hands in his. "Thank you, Olielle. You are a true friend."

"It's no more than we'd already planned, except this time, you've returned as a fully Gifted instead of a shamed dreg. You've earned this."

"I can only hope the people feel the same way."

"They will." Her face fell, and she pulled him into an embrace. "Sil… when I heard the reports that you'd died…"

"Why didn't you wait for me?" he whispered, wrapping his arms around her.

Her eyes turned glassy, and she reached up to cup his jaw in her hand. "I tried. When I heard that you were dead… it was like a knife in my heart. I wanted to wait, but my father married me off as soon as the mourning period was over. It turned out for the best though. Autoro is a good man."

He rested his forehead against hers. "Are you happy?"

A soft smile bloomed on her face, transforming her features until she was the vision of a goddess. Slowly, she lowered her hands until they rested on her belly. "We are."

"Congratulations!" Silvano beamed at her. "May your home and family forever be blessed."

"Thank you." She made a shooing motion with her hands. "Now get out of here. You have work to do!"

6

The next morning, Silvano stood at the edge of the sea and inhaled the comforting scent of seawater as gulls cried nearby. The waves crashed over his boots in a violent caress, greeting their new master. He craned his neck to look up at the sheer cliffs where perhaps a thousand had gathered to watch. From this distance, they were nothing more than tiny specks, but that wouldn't make a difference in a moment. It was time. After this, it would leave no question that he was the rightful ruler of Crystalmoor. He would prove he was strong enough to lead them into the future. A better future for them all, nobility, commoners, and dregs alike.

Wherever his sister was, he hoped she was watching.

The thought brought a smile to his face. He didn't know what game she was playing, but it was irrelevant. He had won.

After visiting with Olielle, Silvano had sent two of his guards to the treasury to retrieve a veritable fortune which he promptly dumped at the feet of the high priest. Miraculously, the priests declared that the sea god had spoken, choosing him to be the Miestryri.

He touched a teardrop of sea glass now embedded between his brows. The ceremony had been painful, just as it was meant to be—a reminder that the Miestryri must be willing to suffer and bleed for his people. The priest had anointed him with seawater, symbolizing his rebirth as Miestryri, shedding his former identity and attachments. A Miestryri must put his people first before anyone else. Afterward, the priests had taken a ceremonial blade and carved his forehead before slipping the sea glass beneath the skin. The Healer had healed it cleanly, leaving behind a permanent symbol of rule. A crown could be taken by force, but the sea glass was bonded to his flesh. From today until his last day, he lived to serve his people.

So why did it feel like he lived to serve the priests instead? He hadn't missed the high priest's saccharine smile, or his parting, "We'll be in touch," the moment the Healers had closed the wound. Somehow, he didn't believe that the high priest would be content with gold and jewels. Though he couldn't imagine what the priest would actually want. Outside of anointing Miestryris, the priesthood stayed out of politics, choosing to live their lives in service to the sea god.

He shook off the concern and focused on the task at hand. There would be plenty of time to worry about the high priest's meddling later.

The sea churned around his legs, and his power swelled deep inside his core in response. It begged to be channeled and used, and he was more than delighted to oblige.

The warm breeze carried a gentle murmur from the cliffs. He took a deep breath. It was time.

Without wasting another moment, Silvano reached his hands to the side, gathering the water beneath him. He was about to do something he'd never attempted before. If he succeeded, his people would talk about this moment for generations to come. If he failed now, he would be shamed in front of his people. He could not fail. When Opal had awakened his Gift weeks ago in Tregydar, it had become apparent why the palace Magi had refused to Gift him as an infant—he was obnoxiously strong. Strong enough to threaten the Order. Strong enough to scare the Head Magi.

Strong enough to claim his birthright.

His blood called to the water. Even now, standing with his boots in the sea, he could almost hear it roaring at him. He was the Master of the Sea, the Miestryri Lei Miore', and it was time his people knew it.

He pulled the streams of water slowly, letting them swirl around him like liquid serpents. His crocodile-skin coat flapped in the wind. He pulled more, feeling the waves rise beneath his fingertips. And still, it wasn't enough. He'd barely tapped into his potential. If he wished, he could raise a tsunami that would crest the cliff and punish the people for their gossip and lies. The thought of that much power gave him a heady feeling. The people were at his mercy. The people were his to protect.

The water swirled faster, spinning around him in a cyclone. He fastened it around his torso like a clamp, allowing it to lift him up into the air. A laugh escaped his lips, and he channeled more water into the funnel, lifting him higher and higher until he was at eye level with those standing on the cliff. The people backed away from the edge, giving him wide-eyed stares. Some sank to their knees immediately. Others looked like they were trying to decide if they should run.

What did they see when they witnessed his power? A conqueror? A savior? A god?

He moved closer to the cliff and stepped onto the rock, lifting the water behind him until it formed a wall. He tilted his head up so the sunlight would catch the sea glass in his forehead. Even if they still questioned him, the authority of being anointed Miestryri should win them over.

"My people, I greet you today, not as a conqueror, but as a servant. You may have been misled by the false rumors and allowed your feelings to get the better of you. Rest assured, I have no intention of harming you—I want to serve you. For too long, we have been separated by class, allowing the poorest to suffer. No more. I want our nation to grow and prosper. A rising tide raises all ships! And with your support, your blessing, I will become the greatest Miestryri Crystalmoor has ever known. Together, we will lead our country into an era of unprecedented peace and prosperity!" He let the words hang in the air as he met the gazes of those surrounding him. A few whispers broke out, but most stayed silent, waiting to see what he would do next. Silvano gestured behind him, releasing his hold on the water. It whooshed back into the sea where it merged with the waves, sending a spray of water in every direction. "The sea has chosen me. Will you?"

Now, the whispers grew louder as the people turned to one another. It was not the reaction he'd hoped for. His heart clenched painfully at the smattering of half-hearted applause. After all that, only a third of the audience stepped forward and knelt at his feet while the rest backed away, exchanging fearful glances. A few stood on the outskirts, arms folded across their chests, glaring defiantly. Silvano's guards noticed and edged closer. The protesters weren't doing anything to warrant being arrested, but it was comforting to know that any trouble they caused would be dealt with swiftly. His eyes drifted to the silver ribbons pinned to their tunics, embroidered with his father's crest—a ship being crushed by a giant squid. His eyes widened, and he shoved through the crowd of retreating bodies to get closer. There was only one person brazen enough to claim the Miestryri's symbol while another claimed the throne—Arianna.

Was she here? Had she finally come to see him?

The sudden anxiety he felt took him by surprise. He'd expected to feel hurt and betrayed. Instead, he wanted her approval.

He had to find her. She needed to know what had happened to their father. If he could just have time to explain, she would understand. She had to. She'd always been aloof and reserved in public, but when it was just the two of them together, her edges had softened. She'd curl up with him on the settees in the castle library, begging him to tell her about the mother she'd never met, so cruelly taken from her. Silvano would kiss her on the nose and cross his eyes, just to make her giggle. When her Gift had manifested, Silvano would help her practice for hours each day, allowing her to buffet him with streams of water until he collapsed to the ground, laughing and soaking wet.

He had to believe that she would support him. She'd always been ambitious, but he couldn't imagine that she'd truly turn on him. If he could just speak with her, she would side with him. They could join forces and make Crystalmoor a better place. He and Olielle had spent countless nights plotting what he they would do together. There was too great a disparity between the nobility and the commoners, and even more of a gap between the commoners and the dregs. He wanted a better life for them all, but there was nothing he could do if their loyalties were divided. If they rejected him.

Unless that's what Arianna wanted.

Maybe she wanted him to flounder without support. Without supporters, she could issue a challenge, and she would unseat him easily.

Silvano motioned to Jax to investigate, but before he could follow, Olielle intercepted him. She'd traded her suvali-inspired gown for

Crystalmoor's more traditional dress. The light green fabric cinched above her growing waist with a pleated skirt that skimmed the bottom of her knees. "That was... well, nothing short of spectacular. When I suggested a demonstration, I didn't expect *that*."

He flushed at the compliment. "That was restrained."

"Phew. Well, if that was restrained, I wouldn't want to see you completely let go."

"You and me both." He gestured to the near-empty area, trying to keep the disappointment from his voice. "Regardless, it doesn't seem to have helped."

Olielle placed a hand on his arm and turned him to face her. She took one look at his glum expression and jutted a finger in his face. "You listen to me, Silvano lei Miore'. The people needed to see this. Arianna has been working the general populace for years. They know her. Did you really expect that you could change the tides in one day? Gaining their support and their loyalty will take time, but you will achieve it. Look at what you just did! You scaled a one-hundred-foot cliff with nothing but the power of your Gift. Your sister can't do that, and they know it."

"But they were scared of me."

"Of course they were! I've known you since we were infants, and what you just did was terrifying. You inspire awe and fear and that's something that can't be faked. Haven't you ever been afraid of someone's Gift?"

Silvano opened his mouth to reply with an emphatic no, then closed it. He *did* fear someone—Mara. Just the memory of her tearing through Order Headquarters, laying waste to everything and everyone in it, was enough to send him into cold sweats. His mouth dried. "That's not exactly the response I hope to inspire in my people."

Olielle must have picked up on his inner turmoil. She reached out and looped her arm through his and offered him a soft smile. "Don't worry. It's a beginning. In time, you will earn their trust. And then, nothing will tear it from you."

"Thank you, Olielle." He pulled her into an embrace and pressed a kiss to the crown of her head. "What would I do without you?"

"Probably flounder about like a fish in the sand." Her eyes sparkled, and she laughed. "Come, it's time you become reacquainted with the nobility. They've been following the memory of a specter for so long that they should be reminded of who their leader is."

He grimaced. "Must we? I see no need to ruin a perfectly good morning."

"Behave yourself." She threw him a sharp look that brokered no argument before leading him toward a group of nobles standing on a shaded terrace. Vines wove through the lattice roof, and the musky scent of the nearby wisteria trees filled his nostrils. A handful of servants bustled about, carrying trays of oysters on the half-shell, prawns, and long-stemmed glasses of champagne.

For a moment, he wished he were just another nobleman enjoying a pleasant morning. The reclining chairs by the reflection pool looked particularly inviting. Children, with their pants and skirts hiked up above their knees, waded in the shallows while their parents scolded them about proper behavior. Judging by their giggles and shrieks, the lesson was sticking as well as water to a duck's back.

At his approach, the men bowed, and the women curtsied. Most were older and had served under his father. It was highly unlikely that they would be on board with the radical changes he planned to make. Silvano didn't understand why Olielle would parade him around this crowd until he spotted a group of men and women his age—the heirs to their parents' fortunes. While they didn't hold any legitimate power yet, they would one day.

He recognized Valeria from the parties he'd attended in his youth, and only Olielle's iron grip on his arm kept him from turning around and walking the other way. Valeria's thick, black hair was pulled into a knot at the crown of her head, and long, seashell earrings dipped in silver trailed down to her collarbone. She stood from her shallow curtsy and smoothed the rose-colored fabric of her gown. Her hand lingered at her waist—no doubt intentionally. "Miestryri, a pleasure to see you again," she simpered.

"I wish I could say the same," he muttered under his breath. Olielle elbowed him in the side, and he quickly said, "And I, you."

"I was distraught when I heard of your death. It's a relief to see you alive and well." Without breaking eye contact, she plucked an oyster from a passing tray and swallowed it down whole, licking the juice from her lips.

Silvano tried his hardest not to gag. "Funny, I seem to recall you wishing I would jump off the cliff after I rejected your advances."

Her responding laugh was forced and just a tad too high-pitched to be natural. "Oh Silvano, you're positively wicked."

"Lady Valeria, show some respect to our new Miestryri. Speaking with such informality is unbecoming to us all," Lord Pierce cut in. Silvano could have kissed him. Lord Pierce had been one of his father's staunchest supporters until a monumental disagreement had fractured their friendship. Since then, he used every opportunity to speak out against the Miestryri, using his wealth and influence as a shield against retribution. In his prime, he'd been a force to be reckoned with when dealing with the Belosian pirates, though old age, too much drink, and the death of his third wife had clearly taken their toll. Regardless, he would make a valuable ally.

Silvano slipped back into the familiar, albeit unwelcome, role with ease and plastered a charming smile on his face. "Thank you, my lord. It's wonderful that you could attend this morning."

"I'm glad I did. It was quite… enlightening."

Not one to be ignored, Valeria sashayed across the veranda. She crowded close to him, running a hand down his crocodile-skin coat. Silvano threw a panicked look at Olielle, who looked like she was trying not to laugh. Valeria leaned forward on her tiptoes. Her breath tickled his ear as she whispered, "Well, I wouldn't have missed it for the world. Perhaps you could return the favor? I'm hosting a gala at my villa this evening, and it would be incredible if you would make an appearance."

"I'm afraid I'll have to decline." He stepped back, putting a more respectable—and comfortable—distance between them. "With the responsibilities of ruling a nation, it's unlikely that I will be free for certain frivolities."

Disappointment flashed across her face. Before she could respond, Lord Adwyn said, "That is a relief to hear. I'll admit I was worried when we'd heard of your return. We couldn't afford to have a reckless Miestryri at such a crucial time, and you have a certain… reputation." His beady eyes squinted until his pupils all but disappeared, making him look like a disgruntled turtle. Silvano would have happily ignored him, except for the fact that Lord Adwyn controlled the largest sea glass export in Crystalmoor. The revenue in taxes alone would be critical for funding Silvano's plans.

Lady Liola, a waspish woman with a vinegar tongue and a penchant for gossip, said, "Indeed. Your escapades are legendary, and not in a good way. If my Ambrose had convinced the sea god's priestesses to go skinny dipping on a full moon, I would have had him keelhauled. If you think…"

Silvano tuned out the rest of her righteous tirade. Valeria, likely disgruntled by his cold shoulder, slipped away to join a group by the pool. Frowning, Olielle tracked her movement. She lowered her voice so only Silvano could hear it. "I know the two of you have a shaky history, but her father owns three quarters of the fishing fleet. How do you think he'll react if she tells him how you've treated her?"

He groaned. Political maneuvering and catering to the whims of sycophants was not how he'd planned to spend his day. That was Olielle's strength, so if she thought it was best, he supposed he'd have to tolerate it. He nodded reluctantly.

"Well said, Lady Liola!" Lord Adwyn waggled a finger in Silvano's direction. "Once a reprobate, always a reprobate, I say. A tiger shark can't change its stripes, after all."

Lord Pierce scoffed, "Well, what else is adolescence but a time for wanton behaviors and mistakes. If we were to judge everyone based on the actions of their youth, I'd wager none would look favorably on you, Lord Adwyn."

"So long as those mistakes won't follow into your reign." Lady Liola pinched her leathery lips together and patted her graying hair.

"I understand your concerns." Silvano held his hands to the side in what he hoped was a reassuring gesture. "But I can assure you that exile had changed me in more ways than one. I truly have the best interests of our people at heart, and I am prepared to do whatever it takes to ensure a future for our people."

Olielle smiled demurely. "I think you'll find that our Miestryri has matured beyond his years, and he will prove to be the greatest leader Crystalmoor has ever known, but he can't do it alone. I'm sure he would be grateful for whatever guidance you are generous to offer."

"Hmm." Lady Liola preened from the praise, then turned a skeptical eye one him. "In that case, perhaps I could stop by the castle so we could discuss some ideas I've had about—"

"That sounds wonderful," Silvano said through a fake smile. "In fact, you should speak to the small council. I have the utmost confidence in their ability to solve whatever problem you have."

"I should certainly hope so. There are so many injustices that must be righted immediately." She pulled a scroll from her handbag and shoved it at his chest. "This is a list of grievances I've compiled against my neighbor. Not only has he installed the most abominable eyesore in his front lawn, but his vile children trampled my prized lavender. I demand recompense."

"Flowers and a fountain? That's what you're upset about?" Silvano asked, exasperated. Olielle covered her mouth with her hand to cover her laughter, but nothing could hide the shaking of her shoulders. "Madam, we have very real problems in Crystalmoor that take priority over petty squabbles between neighbors."

"Well, you could hardly expect the womenfolk to have a head for important matters, my boy!" Lord Pierce chuckled, and Lady Liola swelled like a bullfrog.

"Yes, yes." Lord Adwyn handed a plate of prawn shells to the closest servant and dabbed his lips with a cloth napkin. "You gave quite a stirring little speech, but we both know there was little substance."

"I beg your pardon?"

"All that bit about the disparity between the classes and whatnot." He waved his hand in the air. "You were just giving the people what they wanted to hear. Cleverly done!"

"I can assure you it was genuine," Silvano replied. He felt Lord Pierce's appraising eyes on him.

Lord Adwyn spluttered. "But that's preposterous. The disparity between the classes is what keeps our country strong."

"And what keeps the coin flowing."

"Exactly!" Lord Adwyn snapped his fingers, completely missing his sarcastic tone. "You need to understand that our way of doing things, from business to our social order, is perfect as it is. It's the way things have been done for generations because it works. You'll see I'm right."

Silvano opened his mouth, ready to launch into a proper debate, but Olielle squeezed his arm and interrupted. "Thank you, gentleman, my lady. I think it's time we mingled with some of the other guests now."

Without another word, she led him away. Silvano didn't relax until they were out of earshot, and then it felt as if his body was melting. "Well, that was a disaster."

"Hardly."

He gave her a side-eyed glance, baffled by her cheerful expression. "Did we just participate in the same conversation?"

She rolled her eyes. "If you'd been paying more attention to what *wasn't* spoken to what was, you'd understand. Lord Pierce was quick to defend you against the others, and he despised your father, so he will be the easiest to win to our side. He's halfway there already. Furthermore, he had an iron hammer pinned to his lapel, which means he recently entered into a trade agreement with Aravell. Find out what, exactly, and how you can help him. And did you notice Lord Adwyn's doublet? It's practically frayed through at the collar, and his boots are in desperate need of repair. Interesting, for a man of wealth, isn't it? What you didn't know is that a dozen of his combers were lost in a hurricane six months ago, and fewer workers are willing to work for him when they can collect sea glass for free and sell it themselves. He might not approve of you or your ideas, but perhaps he would be more open to the idea if you were to offer assistance."

"Interesting," Silvano said, already thinking of the ways he could use this information. He couldn't force people to work for Lord Adwyn, but perhaps he could make it illegal to collect and sell sea glass without a permit. And Lord Pierce... what trade agreement could he have made? "And Lady Liola?"

"Is irrelevant. She likes to think herself important, but she's already turned over the majority of her holdings to her son, Ambrose."

"That's unfortunate."

"And why is that?"

He shifted uncomfortably. "About five years ago, I had hosted a party on my pleasure yacht. Ambrose fell overboard, and I might have... left him behind."

"Oh, Sil, you didn't!"

"It was low tide," he said defensively, "and it wasn't my fault that he swims like a one-legged goose."

Olielle closed her eyes and took a deep breath. "I can only hope he has a short-term memory; otherwise, you'll have a lot of work to do."

As they approached the other group, Silvano saw a flash of black out of the corner of his eye. He did a double-take, and caught sight of someone familiar—Mikkal's sister, Michelle. Guilt flooded his body as he remembered why Mikkal had been bribed in the first place. Visiting her should have been the first thing he'd done when Silvano returned to Crystalmoor. Well, late was better than never. He turned to Olielle and extracted his arm from hers. "Forgive me, but there's something I need to do."

"But—"

"Thank you for handling this in my absence," he said, and hurried away before she could protest.

7

Wearing a nondescript cloak, Silvano weaved through the slums in the far reaches of East Rock. Small, stucco houses squatted together as if bracing against a hurricane. An occasional potted plant and brightly-colored doors and windows added a splash of color to the otherwise monochromatic palette, but not even a dozen layers of paint could mask the poverty he saw. A year ago, he wouldn't have glanced twice at the suffering. Though he'd been a dreg all his life, he'd grown up pampered behind the castle walls, sheltered from the horrors of reality. But time and circumstance have a funny way of eroding rosy filters.

He forced himself to look, really look, at the crumpled bodies hunched on the road with empty tins at their feet. At the woman desperately trying to trade a strand of shells for three eggs. At a quick-fingered child who was lucky enough to pilfer a fish from a basket and ran off before he was caught.

How could his father have let things get so bad? He'd seen his share of poverty during his exile, but he'd always compartmentalized it as 'other', comparing it to the prosperity of Crystalmoor. What if things had always been this bad, and he'd just been too blind—too privileged—to see it?

And yet, the people didn't seem downtrodden or broken by the hardships. There was a charge in the air, as if they were waiting for something to happen—expecting it, even. It felt like hope.

His stomach grumbled, and he realized he had missed the midday meal. When he'd caught a glimpse of Michelle at the top of the cliff, he'd been so preoccupied with seeing her that everything else faded into a background of unimportance. She deserved an explanation. It was his fault that Mikkal had left Crystalmoor in the first place, and it was his fault that she would likely never see him again.

The overpowering stench of human waste slapped him in the face, and his boot squished in something suspiciously soft and wet. Perhaps the small council was onto something with their ambitious plans for indoor plumbing. He made a mental note to approve their plans at the next small council meeting. His cry of dismay at the state of his boots drew the attention of too many passersby, and he tugged down the hood over his forehead. It didn't matter if he dressed like a peasant. If someone caught a glimpse of the sea glass, it would identify him immediately and cause... complications. Despite his best efforts, the majority of the lower-class had not been swayed by his demonstration and, if his suspicions were correct, still supported Arianna.

Footsteps thudded behind him, and he peeked over his shoulder to make sure he wasn't followed. He let out a huff when he realized it was just a fisherman returning home from the docks, then chuckled at his own paranoia. It wasn't like he was alone. His guards followed at distance, trying to be inconspicuous. Jax had insisted that they accompany him, though their presence was a threat in and of itself. If anyone recognized them, they'd wonder why the Miestryri's personal guards were wandering the slums.

He walked up to the tiny hovel and knocked on the rotting wooden door. He frowned. Clearly, his father hadn't held up his end of the bargain with Mikkal. Or maybe it had taken all twelve gold coins to pay the Healers for Mikaela?

In Tregydar, Opal had recognized Mikkal immediately from her visions, and as a result, he'd been forced to confess the true nature of Silvano's banishment. He still couldn't believe it was true. The day before he and Mikkal had left Crystalmoor, the Miestryri had approached Mikkal with an offer. Mikkal's niece, Mikaela, had been deathly ill with a growth in her brain. Without Healing, it would have eventually claimed her life. In exchange for breaking his vow as a Shield and killing Silvano, the Miestryri would pay him twelve gold coins—enough to pay an entire team of Healers.

As hurt as he was over the betrayal, he wasn't sure he would have made a different choice. If their roles were reversed and it were Lucinda…

Silvano swallowed. He'd had no idea how sick the girl was, or how desperate his Shield had been. If Mikkal had only told him, Silvano would have ensured they'd have enough resources to take care of the girl. No, he couldn't blame Mikkal. The Shield had been bound by an oath of silence. The fault, in truth, lay with Silvano. He should have paid more attention instead of going out, partying and wasting his life away. Maybe then this wouldn't have happened. Then Mikkal would still be by his side, where he belonged. Instead, he was too caught up in cultivating his image and making plans for when he became Miestryri. It was his fault.

And he'd cast aside his Shield like refuse.

Somehow, he'd have to make it up to Michelle.

The door opened, and a woman with long, dark hair filled the doorway. She twisted a stained towel in her hands before brushing the back of her hand across her forehead.

"Michelle."

"Can I help you?"

Silvano glanced over his shoulder at the near-empty street before pushing the hood back to reveal his face.

Her eyes widened, and she backed up a step, pressing a hand to her throat. "Miestryri," she said, bowing her head—whether out of respect or simply so she didn't have to meet his eyes, Silvano wasn't sure. She glanced over his shoulder, her eyes darting around the street. "Is Mikkal…?"

"No, he's not with me." Silvano grimaced. He was so eager to speak with her, but now that he was here, he didn't know what to say. "He's… well, it's a long story. May I come in?"

She hesitated for a moment, long enough to make him wonder if she would refuse him. Then she opened the door wider and stepped back so he could enter. "You may."

He flashed her with what he hoped was a friendly smile, then stepped inside the one-room home. "I'm glad you could make it to my demonstration this morning."

"I was looking for Mikkal. When I heard you had returned, I had hoped to see him again. But he never came for a visit."

Silvano's nose wrinkled at the dirt floor, the bucket of water in the corner, and a wood-burning stove that would provide heat and fuel for cooking. There were no decorations. No trinkets. Nothing that would suggest this barren room was a home. It wasn't enough. How could she live in a place like this?

Michelle folded the towel and leaned over to set it down by the bucket, then seemed to think better of it. She straightened back up and started twisting the towel again. A thousand questions flitted through her eyes. "I'm surprised he isn't with you."

He glanced at her briefly before he continued taking in the sparse interior. The castle was well-furnished beyond anything he'd truly need. Perhaps he could send his men with proper beds and furniture, at least? It wouldn't be much, but it would make their lives more comfortable. His eyes paused on the single pallet, shoved up against the wall. Only one? Belatedly, he realized that Michelle had asked him a question. "Hmm?"

"Mikkal. I thought he'd be with you." Her knuckles tightened on the rag, and she refused to meet his gaze.

Silvano tugged at his collar and focused on the pallet, finding it equally as difficult to look at her. "Oh, yes. Well, he and I had a bit of a falling out."

Her breath hitched in her throat. "You know then. You know what he did."

"Yes, I know."

She reached a hand out and braced it against the wall to steady herself. Taking a few deep breaths, she closed her eyes as if to steel herself against the news. "Is he dead?"

"No." Silvano debated if he should offer her comfort. She seemed so on edge that even the smallest contact might break her, but at the same time, all ships needed an anchor in a storm. Before he could talk himself out of it, he crossed the small room and took her hand in his. "I couldn't. Not after everything we'd been through together."

Her shoulders slumped, and Silvano could almost imagine the tension flooding out of her body. He felt guilty for getting her hopes up, but she deserved to know the truth. "He's... I couldn't let the betrayal go unpunished, so I banished him from my side."

She tore her hand from his and pressed it against her mouth. Silvano marveled at her reaction. Surely she knew that the punishment for treason was death and mere banishment was a mercy.

"I'm sorry. Truly I am. I realize now that I may have... overreacted." Silvano held his arms to the sides, hoping she would listen to him.

"Why are you telling me this?" Her face grew cold.

"I thought you should know what happened to him. Believe me, if I could go back and do things differently, I would." And that was the truth. No matter what deals his Shield had made, Mikkal had stayed true to the end. If only it were possible to go back and retract his harsh words.

"If you're looking for forgiveness, you won't find it here. Mikkal gave up everything, his whole life, to protect you. He would have followed you anywhere."

"I know... I—"

"Why are you here?"

He swallowed. "Mikkal told me why he did it. No matter what oaths he had to swear, his family would always come first to him. I understand that. Some might say that it made him weak, but I believe that bond made him stronger. When he took that deal, he knew that it meant his death, and he did it anyway. He was willing to die in order to save his niece. In order to protect you."

He waited for her to say something, but she kept her lips pressed shut as she stared at him with judgmental eyes. His eyes darted to the single pallet again. "I had hoped to see Mikaela. To see how she is doing."

Pain flashed across Michelle's face. Then she deflated. She nodded slowly and said, "I'll take you to see her."

***

Silvano knelt beside a tiny grave outside the city. It was under a tree, next to a shallow stream that twisted playfully through the countryside. A pair of speckled warblers sang nearby. Michelle set down a potted daphne and a trowel. After they'd left her home, she insisted on visiting the market first to buy the sweet-scented flowers. When he'd asked again where Mikaela was, her demeanor had seemed evasive. Now he knew why.

Michelle knelt beside him, stroking the grass over the grave as tears trickled down her cheeks. "She was only nine, you know. So full of life, even as death came for her."

His heart clenched painfully. Nine. The same age as Lucy. "I don't understand. What about the Healers?"

She shook her head and picked up the trowel. She gently cut into the soil, heaping the dirt to the side. "Hours after you and Mikkal left, three of the Miestryri's guards burst into our home and took the money Mikkal had given us. They said that Mikkal had stolen it, and they threatened to throw me in the dungeon as well. There was nothing I could do. I sold everything I could, but there was nothing left to pay the Healers. It wasn't enough."

Rage welled inside Silvano. It had been the perfect plan. His father would have told the people that Mikkal had gone rogue. Then, when Silvano's body would have inevitably shown up, his father could have denied any involvement, blaming it on the actions of a single man. A dog turned on its master. His death wouldn't have been traced to the Miestryri.

"She lived two more wonderful months before she went to sleep and never woke up again." Her voice broke and she stared off into the distance.

Silvano carefully pried the trowel from Michelle and took over digging. "Why is she here? Why wasn't she given to the sea?"

"Mikaela never felt the call of the sea. No, this was her favorite place. The sea is too violent and full of power, but her spirit was gentle. Since she was a baby, I would bring her here as much as I could and lay her on a blanket by the stream. She'd spend the whole day playing with the water if I let her. Then, she got sick. She tried so hard to be strong for me and hide the pain, but the sickness was a thief, stealing the light from her eyes. I brought her here one last time, the day she died. By then, she'd lost the ability to speak, and the shakes were so frequent I was afraid she'd hurt herself. But the moment I laid her by the stream… It was like her whole face filled with joy, as if it were the only time she felt truly alive. This is the only gift I can give her now."

Silvano's eyes burned, and he turned his face away from her. When he spoke, his voice was thick with emotion. "I'm so sorry, Michelle."

If she heard him, she didn't show it. She lifted the daphne from its pot and cradled its roots before lowering it into the hole on the grave. Silvano reached over and helped mound the dirt over the roots, patting it down firmly.

He watched Michelle out of the corner of his eye. By banishing Mikkal, he'd inadvertently taken away the last of her family. She was all alone in the slums, and if he was correct, she'd just spent the last of her coin on the flowers. He spoke hesitatingly, "Michelle, I can't imagine what you're going through. Please, let me help you. You don't have to stay in the slums any longer. I can prepare rooms for you in the castle where you will be more comfortable."

"You want to know how you can help me? You've wasted more coin in a single day than most people earn in a year. Twelve measly gold coins would have meant nothing to you." Her face hardened, leaving a bitter shell of a woman left behind. "If you really want to help, you can leave me in peace, Miestryri. I have nothing left to live for except death."

He jerked back as if she'd struck him.

"Go!" Her face twisted into something violent and feral before sobs shook her body. She curled up in a ball as grief took her.

Reluctantly, Silvano stood. He glanced at the tiny grave one last time before turning toward the castle. Guilt wracked his body, making him stumble on the path. It was his fault. That little girl didn't need to die. Michelle was right. If he'd been more aware of the problem, he could have paid for one hundred Healers if need be. All he could do now was vow that it would never happen again. He would take responsibility, making sure that everyone received the treatment they needed to not only survive but also to thrive. It was the least he could do to repay this life, taken too soon.

8

Silvano returned to the castle with his mind in tatters. He stopped by the kitchens for something to eat, but not even the scent of freshly baked bread and steamed shrimp could tempt him. His stomach turned as the weight of his burdens slowly crushed him. How could he keep his hold on Crystalmoor when his own people were suffering? Moving forward, he would need to make radical changes, starting with the small council meeting tomorrow. His proposal would undoubtedly test the strength of their loyalties.

The afternoon passed quickly, and Silvano grew more restless. After pushing away dinner, unable to eat a bite, he decided that a distraction was in order.

If a visit with his father's treacherous advisor couldn't snap him out of this melancholy mood, nothing would.

As he descended the steps to the lower level of the castle, he decided that the dungeons were perhaps misnamed. The word 'dungeon' conjured images of dark, moldy cells, iron bars, prisoners screaming from torture, and a copious number of rats. Instead, prisoners were not starved or beaten. The Miestryris of the past declared the practice barbaric and fashioned the cells for seclusion and relative comfort. The rooms beneath the castle were just that—rooms. Each was fully furnished with a bed, table, chair, washbasin, and a locked door from the outside, of course.

When Silvano was a child, he often wondered why the accommodations were so fine. What would dissuade people from committing crimes if their punishment was a cushy stay in the palace? His father had adopted a particularly terrifying smile and replied that, for the most deserving of criminals, justice was swift and brutal, usually involving sharks of some kind. Now, he realized that his father was simply trying to scare him. Most criminals never set foot inside the dungeons. Justice for petty crimes such as theft was handled by the chief overseer in each zone of East Rock, freeing the cells for those accused of treason, espionage, and sedition until the time of their trial. In reality, it was a genius tactic. Harsh punishments for minor crimes would turn the people against the Miestryri and incite a rebellion. The nobility appreciated knowing that their sons and daughters would not be tortured as traitors for the rebellious thoughts associated with youthful insolence.

He stepped off the stairs and strode down the hall. A guard that Silvano didn't recognize walked by his side. He seemed like a steady sort of man— middle-aged, with a close-shaved beard and a head of tightly-coiled black hair that fit his scalp like a helmet. Desperate to break the uncomfortable silence, Silvano asked, "He seems in good spirits?"

The guard jumped as if startled by his words. Hm, perhaps not as steady as he'd thought. "Yes, Miestryri. He eats all his meals and asks for seconds."

"Does he ask for entertainment?"

"Just a quill and parchment. He'd asked if we could send a letter to relatives outside the castle, but I declined his request. Then he asked for books. He must do little but read because he goes through two a day."

"Hmm... that doesn't sound like a man who's been defeated." Silvano frowned. From what he could remember, Lucan had never been much of a reader. Old age and confinement must have softened him to the hobby.

"Far from it. The way he smiles... it's like he knows a joke that the rest of us miss." The guard grimaced and gestured for Silvano to follow him down a hall to the right. "I don't mean to speak out of turn, but perhaps it would be best to move his trial up."

"I can assure you that it's a top priority. Who has been caring for him?"

The guard spoke slowly, as if he thought Silvano would be upset with his answer. "Only me, sire, and an elderly chamber maid named Beatrice. No one else will go near him."

Silvano scoffed, "Are my guards such cowards that they're afraid of a single, unarmed man? That isn't a comforting thought."

"You misunderstand, Miestryri. They're not afraid of being harmed physically. Lucan deals in secrets, you see, and the rest have enough secrets to drown a whale."

"Secrets?" He tilted his head.

"Alliances, marriages, trade agreements, and the like." The guard shuddered and cast a sidelong glance at Silvano. "The things he knows... it's unnatural."

"So why are you different?" Silvano's eyes narrowed, and he examined the guard further.

Judging by the lack of physical weapons on his person, Silvano assumed he was a general, run-of-the-mill Armis. There was nothing that would make him remarkable. If Silvano passed him on the street, he wouldn't look twice.

The guard shrugged. "I have nothing left to lose."

"Did he threaten you?" Silvano asked, genuine curiosity bleeding into his tone. He had known Lucan his entire life, and the advisor wasn't the most social man. He'd kept to himself, lurking in the shadows more often than not when he wasn't whispering in his father's ear. If he did know as much as the guard claimed, it was as a result of an extensive spy network, and not through his own doing. That could prove useful, provided he could wheedle any information from the swine.

"It's nothing. He can bark as much as he'd like but it won't change anything. He's secure." The guard stopped outside a nondescript wooden door and pulled a ring of keys from his belt. "Here we are."

Silvano waited for the guard to unlock the door before stepping into the room first. The guard let out a sound of protest, but he needn't have bothered. Lucan was no threat. In his prime, the man couldn't wield a butter knife without impaling himself. He doubted Lucan could overpower a guppy, let alone two armed men.

The advisor sat on a wooden chair by the window, flipping through a book. At their entrance, he looked up and smiled. "The prince has come for a visit," Lucan said, sarcasm dripping from his voice. "I'm honored."

"Miestryri now." Silvano shut the door behind him and stepped closer. He returned the smile and tapped the sea glass embedded in his forehead. "I've won."

"Congratulations. Forgive me if I don't bow." Lucan turned to the guard and waved the book in the air. "Davis, a pleasure as always to see you. Please inform Beatrice that the reading material has grown rather dry, and I would appreciate something more... colorful."

The guard—Davis—shot a glance at Silvano before nodding.

Silvano tilted his head to the side and studied the old advisor. He expected to see anger or fear, but Lucan appeared almost bored. More than anything, that worried him. "Aren't you afraid?"

"Are you here to kill me."

"Not today." Silvano clasped his hands behind his back.

"Ah, so it's information you want. How predictable." He set his book down and adjusted the sleeves of his plain, brown tunic so they exposed his forearms, slow enough to be intentional. He sat back in his chair and crossed his legs at the knee. "Very well. Ask what you must."

This was too easy. Silvano's eyes narrowed in suspicion. "And do you vow to answer honestly?"

Lucan's lips quirked up at the corner. "Perhaps."

"That's a no, then."

"Well, it depends on the question, I suppose. You are free to ask whatever you wish, just as I am free to withhold incriminating information."

"I wouldn't put it past you to intentionally mislead me." Silvano reached to the side and called with water from the washbasin on the table. It flowed through the air and coiled around his fingers like a serpent.

Lucan grew eerily still as he tracked the movement. "I see you've learned in your exile. You've grown. You're more cunning than I anticipated."

"And more ruthless, I'd wager." Silvano let the water trickle across the room until it hovered around Lucan's neck like a quiet sea. "With your trial date quickly approaching, I'd think you'd be inclined to answer honestly to barter for a more lenient sentence."

"I'm not foolish enough to believe you'd offer me anything but death, regardless of whether I cooperate or not."

"I suppose it depends on your answers," Silvano said, throwing the advisor's words back at him. This was not going as he'd imagined. He'd pictured Lucan on his knees, begging for forgiveness, desperate to save his own neck. A spark of rage flared as the man stared back defiantly at him as if he were a child in need of chastisement.

A muscle in Lucan's jaw twitched. "I find that I do not trust your brand of justice. Now, ask your questions unless you plan to irritate me to death with circular banter all day."

"Careful, now." Silvano lifted the water until it covered Lucan's nose and mouth. The advisor's eyes widened in panic. The reflex would be to take a deep breath, but his lips clamped shut. "You should treat me with the respect afforded my position."

A minute passed. Then two. Lucan's face turned purple. He reached up to claw at the water, as if that would make a difference at all. The water was *his* to command. He zeroed in on Lucan's exposed wrists—specifically on his father's crest, tattooed on the inside of his right wrist. Its twin, darker and fresher, was inked on the left. Silvano waved his hand and the water splashed to the floor. "Are you in league with Arianna?"

Lucan slumped in his chair and gasped for breath. He wheezed, "I already told you. I serve the one true Miestryri."

"I am the Miestryri, old man!" Silvano pointed again to his forehead.

Lucan was not a stupid man, so there was really no excuse for why he said, "A beautiful delusion, but fantasies rarely become reality, even for the most desperate of individuals."

Silvano's fists clenched and unclenched. He would admire the advisor's backbone if it weren't so utterly infuriating. As it was, he wanted to throttle the man into submission. In the end, he took a deep breath and let it go. The advisor's defiance was inconsequential. The trial would be soon, followed quickly by the execution. The only thing that mattered now was getting as much information from him before he was nothing but a corpse. "What are Arianna's plans? Why hasn't she come to see me yet?"

"You expect me to betray the trust of my master?"

Silvano gripped the chair's hand rests and leaned forward. His voice was dangerously quiet as he asked, "Why not? It appears that betrayal comes easy for you."

"I have betrayed no one." Lucan's chin lifted, and he glared back defiantly.

"I have not come here to debate semantics."

"Good. Then ask your next question."

"Miestryri, I would be happy to ensure that he's more... forthcoming," Davis said, holding his hand to the side and flexing his fingers like he was just itching to manifest his weapon.

"That won't be necessary." Silvano retreated a few paces. He sat on the edge of the bed and crossed his legs, mirroring Lucan's position. Davis had mentioned secrets... specifically about trade agreements. It gave him an idea. He studied Lucan carefully as he said, "I've heard you trade in secrets. What do you know of Lord Pierce's recent trade agreement with Aravell?"

Lucan's face gave nothing away. "Depending on how recent, you would likely know more than I," he gestured around the room, "as I've been sequestered in this box."

"There's no need to be modest. We both know your network is extensive, and a trade deal of this magnitude must have taken months to arrange," Silvano bluffed. For all he knew, Lord Pierce had traded a shipment of sandstone for a lifetime supply of salted pork or something equally as boring.

"Why do you want to know?" he hedged.

"Curiosity, mostly." Silvano asked, keeping his face blank even as his mind raced. If the trade was innocuous, why was Lucan being so tight-lipped? Was Lord Pierce, despite his vocal support of Silvano, working with Arianna? Or did the advisor truly know nothing?

"Many lords and ladies enter into private agreements without the blessing of the Miestryri. It's not illegal." At Silvano's nod, Lucan continued. "From what I understand, Lord Pierce is arranging something special for the navy."

Silvano's brow furrowed. That was not what he expected. "What is it, exactly?"

"I couldn't tell you. If I were in your place, I would ask the admiral. Unfortunately, from what I understand, you have not appointed one yet, and your naval officer is barely out of his small clothes."

He glanced up sharply. "So you do know more than you're letting on."

"Only if you admit that you appointed a veritable child to lead your naval fleet."

He bristled under the criticism. "What he lacks in experience, he more than makes up for in knowledge and enthusiasm. In addition, he's loyal, which is more than could be said for you." Silvano pulled himself up short, realizing he was handing out information that would better be kept quiet. "Why am I even telling you this?"

"What can I say? I'm easy to talk to." He stood from his chair and brushed his trousers. "Well, if there's nothing else, I'd appreciate it if you left. You're infringing on my daily nap. Thank you for stopping—"

"Why did you and my father plot to have me killed?"

Lucan sighed and sat back down, the chair creaking under his weight. "I wondered how long it would take to get to that question."

"Answer it."

"Do we need a reason to dispose of a wayward prince who destroys everything he touches? Do fishermen need a reason to dump chum in the water?"

"You owe me an explanation. I know my father and I never had a close relationship, but did he truly hate me that much?"

"Your father." Something akin to madness flashed in Lucan's eyes. "Aye, he hated you. He couldn't even look at you without—"

"Without what?"

"You don't know how close we came to succeeding." Lucan began to laugh, his voice cold and cruel when he said, "The only reason why you're alive is because of a servant girl's incompetence."

Silvano knew that his father had wanted him dead, but having it confirmed by Lucan's words was a knife in his gut. He didn't understand. What could he possibly have done to earn the Miestryri's wrath?

"The Miestryri made every effort to get rid of you. He shipped you off to Kearar, hoping that you would stay put. Or perhaps you would offend the Rei and be strung up in the desert for the jackals and carrion birds. Instead, you returned wild and untamed. You were a threat, even if you tried to act like a fool. I knew what you were up to. You can't hide secrets from me."

"I don't know what you're talking about."

"Don't you?" He leaned forward in his chair. "I know all about the plotting you and Olielle were doing behind the scenes. She told you about a threat to your life, and she concocted this scheme to present you as a reckless playboy. Maybe that would have fooled the Miestryri, but it didn't fool me. I told him what I'd learned, and he agreed that you needed to be handled. Permanently."

Silvano shut his eyes, not wanting to believe it. Mikkal had told him as much—that his father had planned the assassination. But even now, hearing the truth stung sharper than a stingray's barb. He took a deep breath. He needed to hear the full story.

"We agreed to poison you. Just a dose of Lyspine, which would mimic the wasting sickness. Nothing serious enough to warrant a Healer, who would recognize the poison's effects immediately. You would wake up feeling ill, but no amount of rest would help you improve. Each day, you would grow weaker and weaker until one day, you wouldn't wake up at all. He'd planned to blame it on the fact that you were a dreg, and no one would question it. The night of the banquet, I poisoned your cup, but the serving girl delivered it to the Miestryri instead. He almost died."

"That's why he had you arrested."

"Yes. He was understandably furious and spread the rumors that I'd been trying to assassinate him all along. Not the best course of action, but no one is capable of controlling their emotions at all times, I suppose. Eventually, he paid me a visit, and we formed a new plan. This time, he would handle its execution."

"Mikkal," Silvano said in a flat tone.

Lucan nodded. "Mikkal. It was the perfect plan."

"And yet, after all this, you still haven't told me why. Why did he want to kill me so badly?"

"I'm afraid our little chat is over, *prince.*" Lucan stood and crossed his arms. "Davis, if you would be so kind to escort my visitor back to his rooms."

Silvano stormed across the room and glared down at the advisor. "It's over when I say it's over."

"Feel free to torture and starve me, but I've been more than generous with you," Lucan said as though he were bestowing a great honor on Silvano just by allowing him in his presence. "You won't get me to speak further. Remember, I'm not the only person who deals in secrets."

"What's that supposed to mean?" Silvano backed up a step. Must everyone speak in riddles?

"It must have been difficult to return home, only to find your betrothed married to another man. Tell me, have you visited with Olielle's father since your return?"

"Lord Maynard?" His face scrunched up in confusion. "Why?"

"You might find the conversation… enlightening. Farewell."

Silvano flew from the room before his anger got the best of him. Oh, he would go and pay Lord Maynard a visit immediately. Perhaps that conversation would prove more satisfying than this one had been. Now, more than ever, he needed to know the truth. Why did his father hate him so much, and what did Lord Maynard have to do with it?

Once they were down the hall, he turned to Davis and said, "Withhold his rations for a week."

"Sir?"

"There's no point in wasting food on a dead man, and hunger might loosen his tongue." He took the steps two at a time. "You will accompany me to Lord Maynard's house."

Davis jerked his chin to acknowledge the order and hurried after him.

An out-of-breath guard met them at the top of the stairs. "Miestryri. You must come at once."

Silvano opened his mouth to lecture the guard about giving orders to the Miestryri, but one look at his unnaturally pale face made him hold his tongue. "What is it?"

"A package just arrived for you." The guard nodded at Davis, and they both took positions on either side of him. "It's in the throne room."

"A package from who?" Whispered conversations cut off abruptly as he approached. He noted more than a handful of tear-stained faces as he walked through the arched hallway and into the courtyard. He blinked, allowing his eyes to adjust to the bright sunlight.

"Arianna."

That one word was enough to send Silvano racing across the cobblestones. Jax peeled away from the wall and rushed to Silvano's side. With a gut full of trepidation, Silvano pushed through the courtyard and into the eastern hall. "Is she here?"

"I don't know, Miestryri. I was following your sister's men and only just returned myself. Wait while I clear the room." Jax motioned for additional guards to surround Silvano before racing ahead into the throne room. Unsure what he should do, Silvano followed at a slower place, suddenly afraid of seeing what was causing this grief. His boots dragged on the polished floors. Whatever had happened, somehow, he knew it was his fault.

The two guards at the doors to the throne room bowed, but they did so with deep scowls etched onto their faces. It was enough to give him pause.

At Jax's anguished cry, knew he couldn't wait. Silvano burst through the doors. Jax collapsed to the floor and pounded a fist to the stone. At his left was a melon-sized black bag that was wet at the bottom, as though something had leaked through. His heart thudded in his chest. He couldn't tear his eyes away from it.

"What…"

Jax shook his head. "Mateo."

Silvano didn't want to look. He couldn't look, but how could he not? He reached out a shaking hand and opened the bag, immediately wishing he hadn't. He retched as the stench of rot hit his nose. It was the head of the guard he'd sent to follow Bas. Fresh guilt rushed through his mind. He hadn't even known his name. He swallowed bile and asked, "What happened?"

Jax held up a note. His voice cracked as he read, "Don't follow me again. I'll be seeing you soon, brother."

9

Night had fallen over Crystalmoor, and a sliver of the waning moon glistened over the restless sea. Silvano stood in the throne room, staring at the throne he hadn't dared claim. Carved from driftwood and encased in clear resin, it had stood for generations of Miestryris before him. And he wanted nothing more than to burn it to ashes. Without the respect of the people, it was nothing but an empty chair.

Even with the coerced support of the priests, it wasn't enough. His hold on the country was too brittle. It would be so simple, to just walk over and sit down, but for some reason, his body wouldn't obey. He ground his teeth in frustration and whirled away, clutching the cool stone of the windowsill as if it would steady him. It didn't work. His mind continued to spin as he replayed the events of the past few days. There were so many things he wished he could have done differently.

After Mateo's head had been delivered to the palace, Jax had retreated into his rooms, refusing to eat. Silvano knew that Jax blamed himself for allowing the boy to go on a mission he was wholly unqualified for, but the fault was really his. He should have never sent such a young, inexperienced guard to trail Bas. Judging by the way the guards refused to speak to him outside of mandatory orders and reports, they all blamed him as well. But how was he supposed to know that Arianna would stoop to such measures?

He caught sight of his reflection in a mirror. The skin around his sea glass had grown red and puckered. That shouldn't happen. With every Miestryri before him, the glass had merged perfectly with the skin without scabbing. Had the priests done something to the glass when they crowned him? He dismissed the thought immediately. They wouldn't dare offend the sea god like that.

Or would they?

He glanced back at the empty throne with a deep sense of foreboding and more than a little longing. It was his now, but he no longer believed he deserved it.

"If you want it so badly, why don't you just sit down?"

Silvano jumped and looked toward the sound of the voice—a voice he'd know anywhere. Arianna crouched on the windowsill and scowled at him. The light, musical lilt of her voice did little to hide the animosity that radiated from her posture. She clutched the windowsill, her body coiled as if she were about to launch herself at him. She had a dagger strapped to her thigh, but other than that, she appeared unarmed. He tried to picture her as the child he knew, but all he could see was the blood on her hands.

"No matter what you've done, we can work it out. We don't have to be enemies," he whispered to not alert the guards stationed outside the doors. He didn't want to harm her, but the guards would want revenge.

Her scowl deepened. "Too late for that. Any goodwill I felt toward you vanished the moment your sword pierced our father's heart."

Taken aback by the venom in her voice, he asked, "Is that why you killed Mateo? Because you were upset with me?"

"You were the one who sent him to spy on me."

"Only because I couldn't find you. Why didn't you come to me before?"

"Why? So you could eliminate your competition the same way your eliminated our father? I never took you for the ambitious type."

Irritation burned in his gut. "It wasn't like that. Please, come inside so we can talk about this. We could go down to the kitchens for some refreshments, just like we did as children. There might be some leftover fish pie—your favorite."

"How gullible do you think I am? The second I come inside, you'll call for your guards and throw me in chains. No, there's much to discuss with you, brother, and I'm quite comfortable here." She swung her legs inside and leaned against the stone. Keeping her eyes on him, she drew her dagger and laid it across her thighs.

"Suit yourself," he said, keeping his voice even while he angled his body toward the door. If she attacked, he would run for the guards. Nothing could cause him to raise a blade against his sister. "What did you wish to discuss?"

Her eyes narrowed like she expected a trap. When he stayed silent and unmoving, she demanded, "Step down and renounce your claim immediately."

His eyebrows shot to his hairline. "Why would I do that? I am the rightful heir!"

"Are you? It seems you haven't been into father's study since you came home."

"What do you mean?"

Arianna shrugged. "It doesn't matter anyway. The people clearly don't want you. They showed you as much this morning."

"You were there? I didn't see—"

"You have betrayed them to their core by murdering their leader. You're nothing more than a power-hungry usurper to them now." She spat on the ground and wiped the back of her hand across her mouth.

Silvano brushed off the insult, desperate for her to understand. "I'm not about to give up everything I've worked toward." He took a step toward her with his hands held up to show that he wasn't a threat. "I need your support. We're on the cusp of greatness, Arianna. With you behind me, I could take Crystalmoor into the future. We could expand our trade with Aravell. Imagine having their technology here. We could improve the lives of our people exponentially. Why don't you come to the small council meeting tomorrow? When you hear the changes I'm proposing, you'll understand that all I want is to do the right thing by our people. And if we work together, we'd become the greatest country on the continent!"

"I will not work with the man who killed my father."

Silvano's patience was a brittle strand, seconds from breaking. "He attacked me! What was I supposed to do? Let him take off my head? All I wanted was for him to welcome me home."

She snorted and crossed her arms. "Likely story."

"It's true! There are so many things you don't know."

"Like what?" She quirked a brow like she was humoring him but didn't believe a word he would say.

His stomach plummeted. Even though he knew she would argue with anything he said, he had to try. "When I was exiled, Father hired Mikkal to assassinate me."

"Then why are you still alive?"

"Mikkal had a change of heart."

"That's a convenient story."

"Talk to Lucan if you don't believe me. He confessed to everything."

"I would love to speak with Lucan, but you have him locked in the dungeons."

"It's the truth!"

"Truth is as fluid as the sea, and just as salty." She shook her head slowly. "I can't believe a word you say. I can only see the pile of evidence laid before me. Everything you've done has been for yourself. You mentioned wanting to improve the conditions for everyone, but why? Is it because you truly want what's best for the people, or is it nothing more than a political move to benefit yourself?"

Silvano wanted to rip his hair out. He threw his arms to the side in exasperation. "What do you want from me, Arianna? How can I prove myself to you?"

"Abdicate. Leave the palace immediately with nothing but the clothes on your back. Prove to me that you are innocent by giving up the one thing you've ever wanted. This is your final warning." And with that, she slipped out the window and into the night, letting the darkness swallow her whole. "If you think things are bad now, just wait and see what happens if you don't comply."

Silvano raced over to the window, his knuckles turning white where they clutched the stone, and leaned out over the edge. Where had she gone? Was she still in the castle somewhere? Even if she had truly left, she couldn't have gone far. He opened his mouth to call for his guards, then closed it slowly. Sending armed guards to hunt her down and drag her back in chains would only confirm her beliefs about him. No, he would let her go. But he would also fortify the castle to prevent any more late-night visitors. If Arianna wished to see him, she could come through the front gate and request an audience like anyone else.

10

There was one room in the castle that Silvano hadn't dared enter since his homecoming—his father's office.

Arianna's visit had left him feeling more than a little unsettled. He'd tried going to bed, but he'd done nothing but toss and turn as her words tormented him.

You haven't been into father's study since you came home.

What did she mean by that? Was there something inside he needed to see? A secret message? Or was she simply throwing their childhood in his face?

As children, they were forbidden from going inside. Only once had he broken the rule, and he hadn't been able to sit down for a week. Even now, it felt as though there were an invisible fence blocking the door. Positively ridiculous, considering the Miestryri was dead. It didn't stop him from feeling like he was about to be punished as he pushed open the door and stepped inside.

He lifted his lantern to illuminate the room.

Sconces holding candles melted into stubs lined the stone walls. Portraits of Miestryris hung at regular intervals, their sharp features staring down at him in judgment. A small wooden desk was pushed up against the wall between two arched windows that overlooked the sea. Plans for building new ships for the navy lay scattered across the surface of the desk. Silvano picked one up and set it back down after a moment. Other than basic terminology, he knew next to nothing about ships.

Silvano frowned. What was he even looking for?

He crouched by the desk and pried open the drawers. A telescope. A roll of parchment. Maps. He was about to slam the last drawer shut when a scroll caught his eye, fastened with the Miestryri's seal. He gently lifted it, broke the seal, and unrolled it. He read it. Then read it again.

His world tilted.

"Shh... father will hear you," I hissed at Arianna.

She clutched my hand tightly. "We shouldn't be here. Papa will catch us."

I grumbled and pulled away, wiping my hand on my trousers. The feel of my now-empty pocket stopped my heart. I clearly remembered shoving a frog inside just ten minutes ago, intent on slipping it inside the cook's bread bowl before dinner. She was terrified of frogs, and imagining what her face would look like when she saw it nearly sent me into a fit of giggles. I pressed a palm to my mouth.

But if the frog was missing…

They peered through the crack in the door of their father's office as the shouting started again.

"I'll not have it!" Father's voice rang out followed by a loud crash as something shattered against the far wall.

I craned my neck to peek around the corner, hoping to catch a glimpse of green. If the frog had gone inside, I would be blamed. And punished. It hardly seemed fair. The fact that I had smuggled it into the castle in the first place escaped my logic.

Someone whimpered. "Miestryri, please listen to reason. The people will turn against you if you follow through with this."

"Accidents happen all the time, Lucan. I shouldn't think you'd be squeamish."

"It just seems unnecessary, that's all."

"Are you turning traitor?" his father growled. My ears perked up. I'd hoped for some juicy gossip when I'd convinced Arianna to eavesdrop with me and hearing Father call his advisor a traitor was as juicy as I could imagine. I held my breath and waited to hear something else break, but the room was deathly quiet. I pouted. It would have been exciting to watch the guards drag Lucan away. The man always gave me the shivers.

"Look, a letter arrived from the Rei this afternoon."

I heard a rustle of paper, followed by creaking as his father sat in his chair. A minute of pure boredom passed, and I scanned the hallway, quickly losing interest in eavesdropping. Where had that frog gone? It was nearly suppertime, and we would need to get down to the kitchens to pull off the greatest prank ever.

"Do you think this will work?"

"Yes, and if not, there are other... alternatives we can discuss. Let's not jump to the worst-case scenario immediately."

"Very well. I'll write to the Rei. Please assemble the necessary supplies for the journey."

"Sire..."

"What now?"

I flinched. I hated that tone. When Father spoke in that voice, it usually meant that pain would follow. I wanted to warn Lucan that he was in danger, but self-preservation kept me quiet.

"He'll need a Shield."

"Doesn't that defeat the purpose?"

"He's noble-born. It will look odd if he's sent away with no protection."

"Fine. Fine! Just do it and may the sea god take you. But mark my words, Lucan. He will never be Miestryri."

Arianna looked sharply up at me, but I had stopped paying attention to whatever Father was saying. Just there, a foot away from the desk, was that pesky frog. I sucked in a breath, hoping that Father wouldn't notice, or worse, step on it.

The chair creaked. Heavy bootsteps heading toward the door sent us racing around the corner. We waited until the footsteps retreated, then I grabbed Arianna's hand and pulled her toward the office.

She froze in the doorway. "We can't go in there!"

"We have to! My frog is in here, and father will skin me alive if I don't fetch it." When she didn't budge, I rolled my eyes and said, "Fine, go hurry back to your nanny. I should never have asked you to come with me."

She began to cry, and I almost felt bad. Not enough to apologize, of course. Now, to find that frog...

I hurried over to the desk, crawling on my hands and knees. Where did it go? I knew I saw it here a minute ago. I stood and searched the top of the desk, growing panicked. In my desperation, I knocked a thick, *black book to the floor. If the loud thwack as it landed on the stone floor hadn't made me wet my pants, the arrival of my father surely would.*

"Looking for this?"

I turned around slowly. Father stood in the doorway, holding the frog by the foot, pinched between his fingers.

"Miestryri? Sil?"

Jax's voice made him jump, and the scroll crumpled in his hand. Silvano blinked up at the doorway, half expecting to see his father glaring down at him. He shook off the memory. "Jax? What are you doing here?"

"I saw the light. No one is supposed to come in here other than you, and I thought it might be thieves." He stepped closer. Whatever showed on Silvano's face must have alarmed him. "Are you all right? Should I fetch a Healer?"

Silvano shook his head. "I'm not sick. I… well… read it for yourself." He held out the scroll.

Jax frowned at him, but he took it and read, his face growing paler by the word. "Is this…?"

"Yes. The same day I was exiled, my father took it upon himself to renounce my claim to the throne and named Arianna as the heir apparent, pending the priests' blessing at the ceremony," he said, his voice devoid of emotion.

"Does anyone else know about this?"

"Other than Lucan and Arianna, I don't believe so."

"Good." Jax lifted the glass from the lantern and lowered the scroll into the flame. The edges curled and blackened as the fire consumed it, leaving nothing behind but a tiny pile of ash. "Now, she has no proof. Her entire claim to the throne is over, and if she were intelligent, she'd flee the country. Come, you look dead on your feet, and you'll need some rest before the council meeting."

Silvano nodded. As he turned to follow Jax out of the room, something on the desk caught his eye—a thick black book. On a whim, he took it with him. He doubted he would get any sleep, but hopefully this would prove to be interesting reading material at least.

He had no idea how true that would be.

11

By an unfortunate turn of events, Silvano found himself trapped in the small council room on the same day that Lady Liola came to air her seemingly unending list of grievances. The only thing keeping him in his seat was the fact that he had very real problems to discuss with the council—specifically, with the minister of sanitation. He hadn't forgotten what he'd seen in the slums, and he resolved to make things better for the sake of the people, and not for his own gain, regardless of what Arianna believed.

His newfound altruism, however, was at odds with his overwhelming desire to strangle Lady Liola.

A feeling made worse by the roaring fire behind him. Sweat trickled down his back, staining his finest white doublet. He had serious doubts that it would wash properly. Which servant had decided that roasting the small council was an appropriate course of action? He had half a mind to send him or her into permanent exile in the frozen wasteland of Tregydar.

His fingers tapped on the cover of the book he'd taken from his father's office. The naval officer shot him a curious glance, and Silvano smiled. They had no idea that he was about to unleash a swarm of jellyfish on this meeting.

An hour passed before Lady Liola was satisfied that the council was taking her seriously, then another before she finally left with an extra bounce in her step and the assurance that her neighbor would receive a citation for his numerous misdeeds.

He sighed in relief, dismissing her with all the appropriate remarks. He opened his mouth to address the council, but before Silvano could take control of the meeting, a messenger burst into the room, clutching a missive like it was a bag of gold. He bowed low. "Miestryri, a message for you from Order Headquarters. Head Magi Cadmus sends his regards."

"Thank you." Silvano took the scroll from the messenger. He smiled and brushed his thumb against the wax seal—an eight-pointed star. Then he turned and threw it in the fireplace.

Gasps rang out around the table. The messenger spluttered, "Sire! That was from the—"

"The Head Magi, I'm aware. Thanks to my possession of two fully-functional ears, I was able to understand you the first time you spoke." He tried to hide his irritation. The messenger had likely been raised to believe that the Order was beyond reproach, an organization without fault, designed to benefit the greater good. But Silvano knew better.

"But—"

"Allow me to make myself clear," Silvano said, pausing to make eye contact with everyone in the room. The minister of the people wouldn't meet his gaze. "It would be my greatest pleasure to drive the Order and all its disciples from Crystalmoor."

With a wave of the hand, he dismissed the messenger, who stared at Silvano as if he'd just admitted he skinned puppies for fun. It took all his self-control to not launch into a tirade over the corruption within the Order. But that was an argument for another day. He was about to launch an assault against their deep-rooted beliefs and traditions as it was.

"I believe we've wasted enough time this morning on frivolous nonsense, so let's get down to business." Silvano stood and addressed the council. "First, I would like to give my full support for the sewer project. This is something that has long been needed, and I believe that it will improve the quality of life for all of our citizens."

The council exchanged loaded looks. The minister of sanitation looked particularly uncomfortable as he squirmed in his chair. "By all our citizens, what do you mean exactly?"

"Exactly what I said. Everyone deserves clean water and streets. I would like to expedite construction as soon as possible, starting in the slums. In addition, I would like to put a team together to clean the streets and hand out food to those most in need."

A small tittering of laughter broke out. The minister of sanitation leaned forward and patted the drawings. "Forgive me, Miestryri, but there seems to have been a misunderstanding. The sewer plans were for the nobility and those who can afford to install it in their own homes. This is still relatively new technology in Aravell, mind you. I apologize if I made it seem as though everyone were going to benefit."

He pretended to be shocked by the statement, but it was no more than he expected from the council. It was easy to overlook the suffering of others when you didn't experience it yourself. "You were planning on furthering the disparity between classes by withholding this from the general public?" he asked, hoping to shame them into cooperation.

"Yes, well, when you phrase it that way, it does sound bad, doesn't it?" The minister of sanitation pulled a handkerchief from his pocket and dabbed at the sweat beading on his forehead. "That doesn't change the fact that it's quite expensive. The people can hardly afford to eat, let alone pay five hundred gold pieces to connect their homes up to the new sewer system."

"My father has been beggaring the people through taxes for years, and as a result, our coffers are filled to bursting. Wouldn't you agree, madam treasurer?"

The treasurer looked taken aback to have been addressed, then she scrambled for her ledger and flipped through the pages.

"Oh, that won't be necessary," Silvano told her. "You see, I was going through my father's things early this morning, and I came across something interesting." He held up a black-bound book and watched for signs of recognition. Their blank faces were almost a disappointment. But what had he expected? "It's virtually identical to the one you use, madam treasurer, but you'll find the numbers don't match up. Curious."

"A clerical error, I'm sure."

"A clerical error. That's a funny way to say embezzlement." The room went silent as all eyes flickered between Silvano to the ledger. "Every single person in this room, with the exception of our naval officer and the minister of the people, is guilty of stealing funds from the treasury. To cover up the theft, taxes have gradually increased over the past few years. I'm sure I don't have to state just how serious of a crime this is."

The treasurer paled. She reached out and braced her hands on the edge of the table. Her breathing became shallow and raspy and, for a moment, Silvano thought she might expire right then and there. "Mercy."

"I will gladly offer all of you an official pardon on two conditions. First, you will pay back every copper bit you embezzled from the treasury. Second, you will approve the sewer project for every home in Crystalmoor, and not just the wealthy." When no one raised objections, Silvano clapped his hands once. "Wonderful! I'm happy we could come to an agreement."

The minister of sanitation opened his mouth to say something, but Silvano waved him off. "There is something else I need to present to the council related to this matter."

Everyone sat a bit straighter. Silvano stifled a grin and wondered how long this newfound obedience would last. It would certainly make council meetings more efficient. For the first time, he felt fully in control.

"Recently, it has come to my attention that the people are being denied adequate medical care because they cannot afford to pay the Healers. This ends today. You will create a system where people can take their sick and injured to be Healed."

The minister of the people nodded. "It's similar to the system they use in Aravell. I'm hesitant to offer my support on this matter. Healers are already expensive and constructing care centers will only increase the rates. It could make the cost of Healing prohibitive for the general public."

"You misunderstand me. The Healers will be paid directly from the treasury—a set amount, so they cannot refuse service."

The treasurer stared at him in horror. "You are going to bankrupt Crystalmoor!"

"I am doing nothing of the sort. So far, their taxes have done nothing but line the pockets of the rich, and to fund my father's lavish feasts. To make up for the added expenses, there will be an increased tax on the upper-class."

"You're going to lose the support of the nobility. They've worked hard for their money, and you're punishing them for it."

Silvano walked around the table and over to the window that overlooked the city. "On the contrary. They've accumulated their wealth by exploiting the lower class in underpaying jobs. It's only fair that they pay more. One might even say it's their duty as citizens of Crystalmoor."

No one responded. He wasn't sure if he should feel proud or offended by their fearful stares. "Thank you for your cooperation in these matters. I expect regular updates on your progress. Now, do any of you have matters to present?"

The naval officer raised his hand and pushed back his chair. He walked to the head of the table to address the council. "There is a new development with the navy. Lord Pierce has acquired a new weapon from Aravell. I would like to request an audience to demonstrate what it can do."

Silvano's ears perked up. Is that the trade agreement Lord Pierce had made? Purchasing a new weapon seemed unnecessary, but he would reserve judgment for now. "Is there a purpose to this weapon?"

"Our reports show that the Belosian pirates are getting bolder. Not only are they boarding and assaulting our ships, but they have recently begun landing on our northern shores, pillaging and raiding the villages there."

Silvano rubbed a finger across his lips. "That doesn't explain why Aravell would equip us with weapons. No matter our alliance, I can't imagine any country willingly handing their neighbors something that could be turned against them."

The naval officer nodded. "That was my initial reaction as well."

"And now?"

"Reports from Aravell show that the pirates are doing the same to them. Unlike us, Aravell has no true navy, and the ships they did have were taken by the pirates. They aren't a military people. Any proposed changes must be sent to committees and voted on. I'm sure you can imagine how this could cripple them in war time. Without our aid, they would be wiped out in a year."

"I see." Silvano frowned. Lord Pierce had never shown an interest in the navy before, or any military business for that matter. What had compelled him to enter into this trade?

"If it pleases you, I'd like us to meet tomorrow morning at the cove where our fleet awaits. My force will run a few test drills to try out the new weapon. With your approval, Lord Pierce will acquire more at the earliest convenience."

Silvano's eyes narrowed. "And what does he expect in return for his generosity?"

"Nothing. I understand that family is his motivator in this instance. His daughter and her husband live in Raven Crest, the capital."

"Very well. If there is nothing else, this meeting is adjourned. We will reconvene in the cove in the morning."

12

Crystalmoor's naval fleet was stationed in a man-made cove a half-mile north of East Rock. Silvano surveyed the area as the sailors prepared for the demonstration. The secluded cove offered protection from the violent seasonal storms common to the area but unfortunately, its narrow bottleneck would be a perfect location for an ambush. He resolved to discuss altering the cove to provide a secondary exit at the next council meeting.

Lush flora covered the rocky coast, shielding the cove from the sea-side view. An early morning fog had rolled in, clinging to the sea and lowering visibility. The naval officer, now appointed admiral, had assured him that it would not interfere with the demonstration.

Silvano stood on the prow of the navy's flagship, The Indomitable, which rocked gently on the small waves. A green-faced Jax stood next to him. From the looks of it, he was just barely holding onto breakfast without tossing it off the side. Silvano took a deep breath, relishing the scent of the saltwater. A flock of gulls cried as they flew overhead. He leaned forward, running a hand over the carved figurehead—a kraken. Its tentacles wrapped around the bow of the ship, swirling along the sides which bore the scars of a hundred battles. The Indomitable had led the navy's armada on hundreds of voyages, and it had never once been boarded. Never been defeated.

And this new weapon would ensure victory for years to come. He allowed himself the indulgence of a daydream—a vision of himself at the helm, leading the charge against the pirates that terrorized the coastline. But he wouldn't stop there. Once he had neutralized the threat of the pirates, he would send his fleet east and conquer both Belos and Talos, expanding Crystalmoor's power. All possible because of this opportune trade deal with Aravell.

Six of the new weapons lined up in a row on the starboard side of the ship where a Farber had sawed holes allowing them to poke through. Each weapon consisted of a long, iron tube mounted on a metal stand. It didn't look like much, but it was technology that he could hardly dream of. Lord Pierce had said the cannons had each cost a fortune, but they would be instrumental in defeating the pirates.

Speaking of Lord Pierce, the man himself stood at the stern, surrounded by a group of nobles who insisted on being present for the demonstration. Dressed more appropriately for a ball than a war exercise, they sipped apricot cordial and nibbled on smoked fish on toasted bread to break their fast. Silvano had politely declined their invitation to join them, stating that he wasn't there to socialize. His snub might come back to haunt him, judging by the nobles' outraged stares and loud whispers.

Silvano strolled to the first cannon where the admiral waited with his hands clasped loosely behind his back. A pile of round, iron balls waited at the back of the cannon.

"Admiral." Silvano dipped his head in greeting.

The tips of the admiral's ears turned red. "Miestryri. There's no need for such formality."

"Nonsense. You'll be leading the armada against the pirates for years to come. How will your crew respect you if the Miestryri does not?"

The admiral shook his head. "I don't deserve the title. Surely there were more experienced sailors."

"There were none I trusted more than you." Too eager to suffer through the rest of the customary greetings, Silvano gestured to the cannons and asked, "How do they work?"

The admiral couldn't hide his enthusiasm. His face broke out in a wide grin that made him appear even younger than his twenty-one years. He smacked the side of the cast-iron tube. "We pack firepowder—a recent invention in Aravell—into the bottom of the bore and then load the cannonball. Then, we light the fuse, which ignites the firepowder and fires the cannonball. Picture a row of Saxums launching melon-sized rocks at the enemy, just with fifty times the power and distance!"

Silvano's eyebrows rose. "You think we could get that sort of range?"

"I do," he said confidently. He gestured to the south. "We have a target ship anchored just there, about a thousand feet away. This is a test run. Our goal for today is to test our range and accuracy in the hopes of sinking it. If we can get a clean hit, I'll consider it a victory."

Silvano followed the trajectory. If he squinted, he could just barely make out the outline of the target ship through the fog. If the admiral's crew managed a clean hit, he would be quite impressed. "Well, far be it from me to delay you."

The admiral bowed before taking his place by the helm.

"Positions!" the admiral called.

The nobles pressed closer, eager to see what the weapons were capable of. Their endless prattling and excitable chatter grated on Silvano's nerves. In retrospect, inviting them had been a mistake.

Groups of four sailors gathered around each of the cannons. Using long poles, they packed the cannons with firepowder and cannonballs. "Aim!"

"Fire!"

They lit the fuses and stood back, covering their ears. With a thunderous boom, the cannons fired. Cannonballs sailed through the air before splashing harmlessly in the water a few yards shy of the target. The sailors groaned as they adjusted their aim for the next round.

The admiral nodded as if that was to be expected. "Reload!"

"Fire!"

Another volley of cannonballs launched toward the target. The nobles, who had applauded the first round enthusiastically, now tittered and giggled behind their hands. Only Lord Pierce stood silently, gripping the rail until his knuckles turned white. He squinted out into the fog as the crew rushed to load another round. And another. The piles of cannonballs dwindled, and the sharp tang of firepowder tainted the air. Finally, a single ball hit its mark, blowing a hole in the side of the ship above the waterline. It was far from a fatal hit that would send the ship to the depths, but a cheer rose up amongst the crew as they celebrated the hit nevertheless.

Silvano clapped the admiral on the back. "Impressive damage."

The admiral's grin consumed his entire face. He gestured wildly as he said, "It is. From what I understand, the balls are designed to detonate upon impact. It isn't much, but we'll work on improving our accuracy, obviously. Regardless, I would wager this is a success. With your permission, I would like to experiment with combining our Gifts with the technology to improve the results."

"You have my approval moving forward."

"Thank you. I really think—"

A cry of alarm rang out among the crew moments before the sound of cannon fire reached his ears. A lone cannonball fell short of The Indomitable, splashing harmlessly in the water. For a moment, it seemed like time froze, then pandemonium broke out. Someone rang the alarm bell, and Silvano raced to the bow. The admiral stepped up to his side and lifted a telescope to his eye. He swallowed, then wordlessly handed the telescope to Silvano. He didn't bother looking through it. The source of the cannonball was clear.

Three large ships cut through the fog like wraiths, sailing toward the cove.

Cannon blasts sounded across the water as cannonballs hurtled toward The Indomitable. The nobles screamed, dropping their glasses and plates to the deck where they shattered, sending shards flying. They scrambled for the longboats, slamming into the panicked crew in their desperation to escape.

Silvano knew he should run, too, but his feet were glued to the bow.

"Prepare for attack! Turn the ship to port!" the admiral cried.

The helmsman turned the wheel sharply. The deck dropped from under Silvano's boots, and he grabbed the nearest rope to stay upright.

"Man your positions! Fire at will!"

The crew's inexperience proved costly. They fired off a few useless rounds of cannonballs, but the enemy ships were out of range. Even Silvano knew it was a hopeless cause. If they couldn't hit a stationary target a thousand feet away, they had no hope at double the distance.

The enemy ships edged closer, sealing the entrance of the cove and cutting off any chance of escape by sea. Silvano lifted the telescope to his eye, hoping for a better look at their sails. His eyes widened, and the telescope fell from his hand. It wasn't the Belosian flag—a skull with a dagger clenched in its teeth—on their sails. Each of the vessels bore his sister's crest.

Arianna's fleet showed no mercy as it sent round after round across the cove.

The crew of The Indomitable returned fire, eating through the ammunition until there was nothing left.

An enemy cannonball blew through the mast. Men and women dove out of its way as it crashed to the deck. Cannonballs blew through the side of The Indomitable. Wood splintered, and men screamed. The ship lilted violently to the side. Silvano slid across the deck. Water sprayed up the sides. He clutched the railing and pulled himself upright.

"We're taking on water!"

"Abandon ship!"

Sailors dove off the sides to avoid the carnage. The nobility on the ship were herded onto the remaining longboats.

The admiral spotted Silvano, and his eyes bugged out of his skull. "Miestryri, you must go!"

Silvano drew his shoulders back and stabbed a finger toward the enemy ships. "That is my sister. It should be me who handles her."

"Sire, I respect your wishes, but this is not a fair battle. We are out of ammunition."

As if to punctuate his point, another cannonball blasted through the side of the ship.

He ran to the starboard side and clutched the railing. If Arianna thought she would have an easy victory, she was sorely mistaken. He planted his boots on the deck and raised his hands. He lifted a wave that towered above the ships and thrust it toward the enemy.

He hoped that the water would slow enemy fire, but the cannonballs cut through the water and rammed into The Indomitable. Shrapnel exploded around him, cutting into his skin and leaving trickles of red behind. A wooden splinter the size of his hand embedded into his thigh. He cried out, releasing his hold on the water. The wave flowed harmlessly back into the sea before it reached Arianna's ships.

Jax tackled him to the deck as a cannonball flew through the spot where he'd been standing. The air whooshed from his lungs when he hit the deck, and pain flared in his skull. Spots clouded his vision, and he gave into the darkness.

13

Someone was tugging on his leg.

Silvano groaned and tried to sit up, but blinding pain in his thigh made him fall back down. His head throbbed when it hit the soft ground. Soft. Why was he laying on something soft? Where was he? He kept his eyes squeezed shut and reached out, feeling the ground around him. Sand? What happened to the—

The memories came rushing back. The Indomitable. The cannons. His sister's ships.

"Lie still, Miestryri."

"Jax?" Sand coated his tongue and crusted his teeth. He turned his head to the side and spat. Blinking, he opened his eyes and his surroundings came into focus. They weren't in the cove anymore.

Dense cover surrounded them, so thick he couldn't see the sea, but the faint screech of gulls and the sound of water crashing on the shore told him they were close. Jax knelt by his side, tying a strip of cloth tightly around his thigh. "What happened?"

"We lost," Jax said bluntly, though he kept his eyes averted. "Somehow, your sister's fleet was equipped with even more cannons than our own. It was a bloodbath. We and the nobility were able to escape in time, but it was a close thing."

Silvano pressed his palms to his temples. Everything… gone. He glanced over his shoulder. The nobles huddled together, dripping wet, looking lost and confused. A few sported minor injuries, but nothing that would slow them down for long. "The admiral?"

"Dead. After evacuating the crew, he chose to go down with the ship."

He hadn't known the man long, but the admiral had already earned his respect. He would have had a wonderful career, had he survived. Silvano felt a flare of remorse. "Who is in charge of the navy now?"

"No one, sire. The fleet has been captured."

The weight of what he said slammed into Silvano. His head snapped up and he gaped at Jax. "All of it?"

Jax nodded. "Every last ship."

"We must reclaim it immediately. Help me up." He reached his hand toward Jax, who clasped his wrist and pulled him to his feet. Silvano tested his leg, leaning weight onto it. He gritted his teeth and took a few steps. The pain nearly made him collapse, but he couldn't afford to rest. "I'll need a team of Irrigos and Ignises. I'd rather burn the fleet to the watery depths than see them under her control."

"Miestryri, with respect, my duty is to keep you safe." Silvano opened his mouth to protest, but Jax cut him off. "We need to get you back to the castle immediately. Now that the fleet has been taken, East Rock will be her destination. We must fortify it against attack."

He nodded reluctantly. It killed him to abandon the navy but losing the capital would be even worse. What he didn't understand was how Arianna knew they'd be in the cove this morning. And where had she gotten the cannons? The only thing that made sense was... His eyes landed on Lord Pierce, who stood at the back of the group.

"Lord Pierce." Silvano took a shaking step forward. He placed a hand on Jax's shoulder to steady himself before puffing out his chest. His voice rang out. "Just how long have you been working for Arianna?"

The nobles gasped. Lord Pierce glanced over in apparent surprise, but Silvano knew better. It was the only thing that made sense. He had arranged the trade for the cannons, and he had close friends in the council. He had more than enough opportunity, but why? What could have possibly motivated him to commit treason?

"Have you nothing to say in your defense?" Silvano asked, hoping he was wrong. It was incomprehensible that one of his strongest supporters was secretly working behind the scenes to undermine him. When Lord Pierce refused to speak, Silvano said, "Jax, take Lord Pierce into custody. We'll take him back to East Rock for questioning."

At Silvano's declaration, Lord Pierce's lip curled. He struck his chest with his fist and jutted his chin upward. "Long live the one true Miestryri!"

Before Jax could stop him, Lord Pierce slipped something in his mouth and swallowed. Within seconds, he collapsed to the ground, mouth frothing. Jax cursed under his breath. He raced over and pressed his ear to Lord Pierce's chest. A few seconds passed, then he shook his head. "He's gone."

Silvano lifted a fist to his mouth and bit down. He turned and let out a strangled cry. Lord Pierce was a traitor. He'd obviously orchestrated the entire morning, from gifting six cannons to the navy while smuggling many more to Arianna. Now, she controlled the fleet, leaving him with nothing. All his dreams of conquering the sea crumbled like sand through his hands.

He took a deep breath. No matter how dire the situation, he couldn't afford to fall apart right now. Jax was right. He needed to get back to East Rock before Arianna did.

***

An hour later, Silvano limped through the streets of East Rock and up to the castle. Blood had soaked through his makeshift bandage, and the throbbing in his head threatened to render him unconscious. He wanted to go straight to the small council, but Jax insisted on finding a Healer first.

He'd already sent the Nobles to their homes, sending each with two guards to ensure their safety. What he hadn't said out loud was that he couldn't trust a single one of them. If Lord Pierce had betrayed him, any one of them might have as well. Until their loyalty was proven, he would keep them all on a tight leash.

"Sil!"

Silvano's eyes snapped to the entrance of the castle where six guards waited with Olielle standing between them. She flew down the steps and wrapped her arms around him. One of the guards tried to pry her away, drawing his cutlass. "Put that thing away before you kill someone, you ignorant seabass. *I'm* not going to hurt him." To Silvano, she said, "You're bleeding! What happened?"

He returned the embrace, burying his face in her shoulder. "Ambush. Arianna took the fleet."

"What? How?"

"Lord Pierce was a traitor."

"Pierce?" Olielle gasped and pressed a hand to her mouth. "Sil, I'm so sorry. I had no idea that he was false, I swear it."

"I know. You're one of the few people I can trust now." He pulled back and stared her in the eyes. "Don't ever betray me."

"Never," she swore. "Let's get you inside and send for the Healer."

With an arm slung over their shoulders, Silvano let Olielle and Jax help him up the stairs, though he protested the former, saying a pregnant woman shouldn't exert herself so much.

She rolled her eyes and barked out a laugh. "I'm pregnant, not terminally ill. The exercise will make the baby stronger."

"But if anything happened…"

She stiffened and pulled back. "Sil, there's something you need to know."

Something about her tone set him on edge. "What is it?"

Her eyes tightened as if she were worried that the news would upset him. "While you were away…"

A guard raced into the room as they stepped inside the castle doors. "Miestryri, Lucan escaped."

Silvano stumbled. He gaped in horror at the guard. "What?"

Olielle took his hand in hers and turned him to face her. "That's what I was going to tell you. There was a riot in the market this morning, which diverted the guards from the castle. The timing was too perfect to be coincidental. We think they planned the rescue while you were away, and security was lax."

"And if I'd died during the attack, all the better." He exchanged a grim-faced look with Jax. Maybe that had been Arianna's plan. By eliminating her competition during the attack, no one would have stood in her way to claim the throne. The priests would have had no alternative but to anoint her in his stead.

"We found this in his cell." The guard held out a book. Silvano recognized it as the one Lucan had been reading when he visited.

Silvano took it and opened the front cover. A scrap of paper slipped out and floated to the floor. Jax picked it up. His face tightened, and he handed it to Silvano. *Your move.* He crushed it in his hand and swore. He knew there'd been something off about the number of books Lucan seemed to be reading. He wasn't reading them at all. He was smuggling out messages to the rebellion under their noses. But he hadn't been working alone. "Where is the chambermaid, Beatrice?"

"Missing."

"And Lucan's usual guard, Davis?"

"Dead, sire."

"They can't have gone far. Send out search parties to find him. Take extra guards and do not underestimate them. It's clear my sister is clever, and she will stop at nothing to see me unseated."

Silvano let Olielle lead him to his chambers to wait for the Healer. How had everything fallen apart so quickly? Just when he'd felt that he was gaining control of Crystalmoor, something happened to cut his legs out from under him. He thought of the last conversation with Lucan. The advisor had asked if he'd gone to visit Lord Maynard yet. It might be nothing more than a distraction, but something told him that he should speak to Olielle's father soon.

14

The next morning, Silvano waited outside a white stucco mansion with arching windows and a walking path that serpentined around the house to the landscaped back yard. Creeping vines grew up the sides of the building, making it look like the house had emerged from the wild fully formed, rather than built by hand. A smile came unbidden to his lips. Olielle had always loved the vines and almost whimsical beauty of her childhood home. They would spend hours wading in the pond behind the house, skipping stones and trying to catch tadpoles and minnows.

If only they could go back to those simpler times.

He rapped on the door and waited until a servant answered. The servant led him through the house and into the study. Lord Maynard sat in his wheeled chair by the window. Silvano's eyes went habitually to Lord Maynard's missing leg—amputated at sea after a botched assault on the pirates—before coming to rest on his hardened face. If he'd noticed the staring, he didn't show it, and Silvano knew better than to bring up the injury that had resulted in Maynard's premature retirement from the navy. He was satisfied to see that the idle years hadn't changed him much, apart from a larger potbelly and an ample number of gray hairs.

"Miestryri, I was not expecting you." He scratched the graying whiskers on his chin.

Out of a lifetime of habit, Silvano fidgeted and bowed his head in respect. "I apologize for not sending word ahead, but I had an urgent matter that could not wait." He tilted his head toward an empty chair, expecting Maynard to ask him to sit. He didn't.

"I see. If you're asking me to annul my daughter's marriage, I'm afraid you'll leave disappointed."

"No, no. Nothing of the sort. Olielle seems content with her new husband, and I will not be the cause of her pain by separating them. Speaking of which, it seems as though congratulations are in order."

Maynard relaxed infinitesimally, and his face broke out into a wide smile. "I'm looking forward to having little ones running around here again."

"I imagine it's too quiet in here now."

"It is. Still, I can't deny that the quiet has been refreshing. I'll never tell Olielle this, but the two of you wore me out." He chuckled under his breath. "So, what can I do for you?"

"I have questions of a somewhat political variety."

"Well then, I believe this discussion requires a strong drink. Religion and politics should never be discussed sober. Jenny!" he called as he wheeled himself behind his desk.

"Oh no. There's no need to trouble your servants." Silvano held up a hand and walked over to the beverage cabinet. "I'm happy to pour it myself."

"Good man. No doubt you'd like as few ears listening in as possible." Maynard's lips twitched.

"Shrewd as ever. Now I know where Olielle gets it from." Silvano pulled a decanter of vintage red and two glasses from the shelf. "Is the red okay, or would you prefer a white?"

"The red is fine, so long as it wets my throat all the same."

"A man after my own heart." Silvano poured the glasses to the brim and carried them over, holding one out for Maynard. "I would appreciate your discretion today. This is somewhat of a... delicate matter."

"Consider my interest piqued." He took the glass from Silvano and took a long drought, licking the excess liquid from his lips. "What can I do for you?"

"Before I begin, I must know—and I'm trusting your word as a gentleman here—are you allied with Arianna and Lucan?"

"Your sister and the Miestryri's advisor? Over my dead body! I don't have anything against your sister personally, but Lucan is an eel. I wouldn't trust him to lick the Miestryri's boots, let alone help run a country."

Silvano took a polite sip. "It has recently come to my attention that my father named Arianna heir, rather than me. Lord Maynard, you were my father's closest friend. Ever since you were boys, you were rarely apart. No one knew his mind better than you. Why?" His fingers tightened on the glass. "Why would he name my sister his heir when I am his eldest child?"

Maynard sighed and ran a tired hand down his face. "I knew it was only a matter of time," he said so softly, Silvano wasn't sure he'd heard him correctly. A crease formed between his eyebrows as he examined Silvano. He pressed a fist to his lips and nodded. "You should know. After all this time, you deserve to know the truth. The reason why Arianna was named heir, and not you, is because you are not his son."

The world fell from under Silvano's feet, and the glass dropped from his hand to shatter on the floor, spraying wine everywhere. Lord Maynard was shouting something, but Silvano couldn't hear a single word, as if he were speaking underwater. Silvano reached out to steady himself. "I don't understand."

The servant, Jenny, bustled into the room and helped him to a chair. She knelt down of the floor to clean up the glass, but Lord Maynard waived her away. "Shut the door and stay away until I call for you." When her footsteps faded, he asked, "Are you going to faint on me, boy?"

The address snapped him out of his stupor. "No."

"Good. Because you'd be laying there until you came to." He patted the stub of his leg. "You'd better have a seat. I expect you want to know the whole story."

Silvano didn't remember walking across the room or sinking into the chair, but he ended up there all the same.

"Arnoux and Emilio were brothers. Arnoux was the oldest by three years, and while many expected him to follow in his father's footsteps as the next Miestryri, he wasn't cut out for the responsibility. Where Emilio was aggressive and relished battle, Arnoux preferred to stay home, spending more time in the gardens or in the sea than in the war council. Though his Gift was more powerful than any we'd ever seen, he couldn't stomach using it for violence. The Miestryri favored Emilio and showered him with praise and attention. He made a match, betrothing Emilio to a woman of extraordinary beauty and grace—Neva."

Silvano's head snapped up at the sound of his mother's name.

"Years passed, and Emilio grew from adolescence to manhood. He spent more time at sea, battling the pirates and making himself into a legend. While he was gone, Arnoux and Neva developed a close friendship. Then the friendship blossomed into something more romantic. You only had to be in the same room for a moment before their love suffocated you. Emilio was too busy with his conquests to notice that his betrothed's affections had been stolen. One day, Emilio returned from a voyage to find his Neva pregnant with his brother's child. In a fit of rage, Emilio swore vengeance. The betrothal had been broken and our laws were clear. Emilio had every right to kill his brother and claim his bride. Neva pleaded for Arnoux's life. She swore that she would be faithful to Emilio as long as they both lived if he spared his brother, sending him into exile instead. Emilio agreed, but he demanded that she take herbs to end the pregnancy and rid her womb of his brother's spawn. Neva refused. She told him that if he forced her, she would fight him for the rest of her life. Each moment of every day, she would make his life miserable, and if she had the opportunity to escape, she would take it."

Silvano leaned forward, resting his head in his hands. His chest tightened, and his body went numb. It couldn't be true. It just couldn't. And yet, it made a certain amount of sense. Why his father—no, not his father—had despised him from his earliest memories. As if understanding his inner turmoil, Maynard offered him a tight smile and slid his glass across the desk. Silvano picked it up and downed it in one mouthful, relishing the burn.

Maynard continued, "They were married the next day. Lucan advised Emilio to keep the pregnancy a secret if he wanted to become Miestryri after his father. The people would not respect a cuckold. He planned on sending you away with your father into exile the moment you were born, but Neva took one look at you and fell in love. She would not be separated from you, not for a moment."

"Why?" Silvano whispered, the sound little more than a gasp in the wind.

"Because she loved you. And the more she loved you, Emilio despised you equally, for you reminded him of his traitorous brother. It wasn't so bad when you were a child, but as you grew, it became clear you inherited your father's personality as well. When your mother died, you lost her protection. The Miestryri sent you to Kearar, hoping that you would die there, or perhaps wed the Rei's daughter. When you returned, whole and healthy, he and Lucan resorted to desperate measures."

Silvano shook his head slowly. "You knew."

"I did."

He frowned, then lifted his gaze slowly. "Then... why did you agree to a betrothal between me and Olielle? If you knew that Arnoux was my father and that I'd never inherit the throne, it seems like a poor move on your part."

"That had little to do with me. Neva and my wife were the best of friends, and it was their wish that we unite our families. They had the agreement drawn before the two of you were out of swaddling clothes, and once it was signed, not even the Miestryri could break it. I'll admit, when you were exiled, I seized on the opportunity to marry her into a more suitable arrangement."

"I can't blame you for doing what you thought best for Olielle. I doubt you were happy about her being tied to a dead man with no claim to the throne," Silvano said bitterly.

Pity flooded the Lord's face. "This must be a lot for you to take in."

"A lot for me to take in?" His laughter sounded hysterical even to his own ears. "I just lost the navy to my sister, discovered a man who I'd thought was an ally was actually a traitor, and a dangerous prisoner escaped from the castle dungeon. Now, I find out that my father wasn't actually my father. That my uncle sired me before being banished to gods only know where. Where is he? Is he still alive?"

"I don't know. The last time I saw him was before you were born when he boarded a ship heading east."

"He could be out there, somewhere." Silvano stood abruptly, his chair screeching across the wooden floor. The walls closed in around him. He almost ran from the room, but a thought stopped him short. "Who else knows about my parentage?"

"Only the Miestryri, Lucan, and myself."

"Swear yourself to secrecy."

Lord Maynard huffed, looking offended. "I've managed to keep my lips shut for the past twenty-six years."

He slammed his palms down on the desk and leaned forward. "Swear it!" In the back of his mind, he knew he was being unjustly harsh, but his emotions had gotten the best of him. Maynard leaned back in his chair, showing real fear for the first time. Silvano couldn't help but feel ashamed, and he couldn't bear to meet the man's eyes.

"I swear. I will not tell a soul what I've told you today."

"Good." Silvano paused at the door. "Keep it that way."

15

That afternoon Silvano perched on the edge of his decidedly uncomfortable throne. His shoulders sagged under the weight of the revelation. One hand lay limp in his lap, while the other traced circles around the sea glass in his forehead. He was an imposter. A usurper. A lifetime of planning and scheming for nothing. He had never been the heir —merely a fatherless parasite. After everything he'd been through, his sister was truly the one who was meant to be Miestryri. Arianna. The one true Miestryri.

He thought back to Opal's prophecy when he'd left Tregydar. She'd told him to reclaim his birthright. Blinded by ambition, he'd took that to mean the throne. But if his father was really the

Miestryri's brother, Silvano was meant to be her right-hand man. Her advisor. Her protector.

Instead, he was her enemy.

How could he have botched this so spectacularly?

He had only one choice left. He would abdicate the throne and turn over the control of Crystalmoor to Arianna. Then, provided she allowed him to live, he would go back into permanent exile.

Jax walked over and stood at his left hand. "Are you okay?"

Silvano swallowed his guilt. He'd barely spoken to Jax since returning from Lord Maynard's house. He should tell him the truth about his parentage, but fear stopped his tongue. What if after learning the truth, Jax abandoned him? It was the intelligent thing to do. Sooner or later, Arianna would succeed, and when that happened, Jax could be executed as a traitor right alongside him. Keeping this secret was cowardice. "I feel like all my dreams, my ambitions, have been burned to the ground. What do I do now?"

"Are you asking as my Miestryri, or as my friend?"

Silvano let out a humorless laugh. "I'm not Miestryri. I can't be."

A commotion in the hall, followed by shouting, drew his attention. The door burst open and a man walked inside. "I beg to differ."

Jax stepped in front of the throne, taking on a protective stance. Silvano shot out of his seat at the unfamiliar voice, his hand going to the hilt of his sword. The man was average height and painfully thin. His silver robes hung off his body like curtains. His white hair was cut bluntly at his jawline, heightening the sharpness of his cheekbones. He carried himself like a man in authority, someone who was used to being obeyed without question.

Every hair on Silvano's body rose. There was something about the man that felt wrong, like a film of oil on water. "And who are you supposed to be?"

A red-faced guard ran into the throne room a moment later, wheezing as he announced, "Head Magi Cadmus requests an audience."

"Requests? Hm… that's a tad bit politer than I would phrase it. Demanded is closer to the truth." Cadmus stopped five feet away at the base of the dais. Though Silvano was taller by several inches, he got the sense that Cadmus was staring down at him.

He stifled a shudder. "And why should I grant you an audience? The Order has no authority here.

Crystalmoor still holds sovereignty, and I am still the Miestryri."

"I'm glad to hear it. I would like for you to remain Miestryri."

That pulled him up short. He squinted suspiciously at the Head Magi. "Why?"

Cadmus studied him intently, as if he could see through his flesh and down into the bone. Silvano resisted the urge to pull his clothes tighter around him. Then, Cadmus smiled like a crocodile with a meal in sight. "Let's just say that it would be a mutually beneficial arrangement."

"I can't see how it would benefit you at all." Silvano clamped his lips shut before he revealed that Crystalmoor was in chaos. Arianna and her sharks were already circling the carnage, and the last thing he needed was to invite more. It would turn the civil unrest into a feeding frenzy he couldn't hope to survive. He changed tactics, turning the focus on his deep-rooted hatred of the Order. "Just two months ago, my companions and I launched an offensive attack on the Order which did not end well for you, if I remember correctly. On a personal note, I have little incentive to form an alliance with the Order. The Magi left me a dreg while the Tregydarian rebels Gifted me."

"Your attack was nothing more than a small hiccup in the grand scheme of things. My disciples had the mess cleaned up within a week. And as for your Gifting... I allow my Magi a certain number of... let's call them freedoms, when it comes to such matters. You, Silvano Lei Miore', were never meant to be a dreg, but the Magi stationed here was bribed to refuse your Gifting."

"What?" Silvano's fists clenched. "You lie."

"I most certainly do not." Cadmus pulled a scroll from his robes and held it aloft. "This is a correspondence I received twenty-five years ago from Magi Phillip who detailed the arrangement he made with the Miestryri and his advisor. Not only was he compelled to bind your Gift with the suppressive elixir, but he also gave you a Deleo to further suppress your abilities."

Silvano's hand went to his neck where the Deleo had hung for over two decades. He'd thought it was a gift, but Opal had recognized it for what it was. She'd taken it from him and had it destroyed. Days later, his Gift had been awakened.

Jax took the scroll from Cadmus and read it, his face paling. "It's true, Miestryri."

"Now, I understand that you have... an unfortunate history with the Order, but I believe we can put that behind us and move forward as allies."

Silvano sank back into the throne. The Head Magi's presence made little sense. Least of all his desire to form an alliance. A dozen questions flitted through his mind but the one that finally escaped was, "Why me?"

"I respect power and influence."

"The power I have tenfold, but influence? Hardly," he scoffed. "You'd only have to sit through five minutes of a council meeting before you realized it."

"You're too modest. Did you not win approval for not one, but two, highly ambitious projects?"

In the back of his mind, Silvano wondered how Cadmus knew about that. Did the Order have spies in the small council as well, or was his knowledge a byproduct of his Gift as a Magi? Still, he couldn't take credit for that victory. He shook his head slowly. "That was achieved through threats and blackmail, not my charming personality. It seems I make new enemies on a daily basis."

"Curious. Would you consider Mara to be an enemy?"

Silvano glanced up sharply. "I'd say my feelings about her are irrelevant."

"Indeed. Yet the fact that you watched her get captured and haven't yet mounted a rescue tells me everything I need to know. You're afraid of her, aren't you? When you close your eyes at night, it's her face you see, tormenting your nightmares.

You're terrified because you finally saw her lose control, exposing herself for what she really is."

Sweat beaded on his forehead, and he clutched the armrests on the throne. Out of the corner of his eye, he saw Jax throw him a curious look. He squeezed his eyes shut as the memories flooded through his brain. He whispered, "A monster."

"The world is full of monsters, Silvano Lei Miore'. Let me help you defeat yours."

Silvano pulled himself from the unending torment and fixed Cadmus with a hard stare. The Head Magi had a talent for words, and obviously had no qualms about playing a man's fears against him. He couldn't afford to be played into a bad deal, no matter how desperate he was. "And what would you get out of this arrangement?"

Cadmus jerked back, apparently taken off guard by the blunt question. "Excuse me?"

"You're a powerful man." Silvano waved his hand in his direction. "I doubt you would do anything for free out of the goodness of your heart. So tell me, what would you want in return"

"Do you know what I find interesting? You remind me of myself when I was younger. We have similar tragic family histories, you and I. My mother abandoned me, and my father was executed for consorting with a Seer. The man who raised me, my grandfather, was a harsh, unyielding man. I tried so hard to please him, desperately seeking love from a man incapable of the emotion. Each misstep was punished swiftly, and brutally, until I learned not to fail. When he died, and I inherited the mantle of Head Magi, I thought I could do better. I wished for a better future for the Order, just as you hope for a better future for Crystalmoor. A mistake, I soon discovered. If I offered my disciples an apple, they stole the whole bushel. They did not fear me, and so they did not respect me. Without that foundation, you have only the illusion of control." Cadmus edged closer, pinning Silvano with his stare like a predator. "You ask what I would gain in return? Obedience. My disciples will eliminate your rebellion and unite Crystalmoor under your control, much like they aided Rei Tomar when his sister was mounting a coup. In return, you will pledge your loyalty to me."

Silvano swallowed, feeling suddenly small. "And if I refuse?"

Cadmus smiled cruelly. "You're an intelligent man, are you not? One thousand of my best disciples are stationed outside the city, awaiting my signal. If you choose to throw away my generous offer, they will kill every last man, woman, and child while you watch, powerless to stop it. Then I will tear down your precious city and wash it into the sea until there is no evidence that it ever existed. And then, we will travel to every city, every village, and every hovel, reducing them to rubble and ash. Only once you have lost everything dear to you, I will end your pitiful life. Like Seralle, Crystalmoor will fade into oblivion, and your name will never be spoken again, except when whispered as a curse from fearful lips."

Silvano trembled. "You are alone and unarmed. Defenseless. I could have Jax run you through right now."

Cadmus seemed unconcerned by the threat. "He won't. Do you want to know why? Because he knows the truth of my words. He sees you, a broken man with no hope—a dead man walking—someone who has already given up. Pitiful. I offer you an opportunity to not only stay in power, but to turn your vision for Crystalmoor into reality."

Jax refused to meet his eyes. Silvano let out a breath, realizing that he'd been trapped. "So you're saying that I have no real choice."

"You always have a choice. It's just that some are more lethal than others."

"Fine. I accept your terms," he spat. "If you can defeat my sister's rebellion and unify the country, I will swear my obedience to you."

"Good." Cadmus dipped his chin once. As he was turning to leave, he said, "Oh, one last thing.

I've learned to not take men on their word alone. Words are, after all, as plentiful as sand and equally as worthless. So, when I return to Order Headquarters, I will require a token of your loyalty to ensure you will not break faith the moment I leave."

A horrible suspicion sprung to mind. "What kind of token?"

"You already know. A pleasure doing business with you. We'll be in touch."

Cadmus swept from the room without another word. Silvano collapsed, his head in his hands. What had he just done?

16

One week. That's all it took. One week for the Order to sweep through East rock and wipe out the rebellion. One week to successfully unite the people under Silvano's rule. He should have been overjoyed with the results, but he couldn't help but feel sick. How had the Order done it? Perhaps it was better not to know.

And Cadmus... Silvano's loyalty wasn't something he trusted on word alone. And now it was time to pay the price.

His long-time friend, Tomar, the Rei of Kearar, had entered into a similar agreement when his sister, Tamara, had attempted to seize control. After the Order had wiped out her supporters, unifying Kearar under Tomar, the disciples had taken his oldest son, Tamil, as a hostage. And now they would do the same to him.

Silvano's feet were leaden when he paused inside the natural archway of a hidden inlet. For generations, children would come here to splash in the shallows. The warm water—a few degrees warmer than the sea—reached his knees as he waded inside. Sea turtles swam lazily by, weaving through the brightly-colored coral, munching on seaweed as they went. And there, up ahead, was Lucinda, stroking Glass in the bright afternoon sun.

He hesitated, watching how peaceful and happy they looked, playing as though they didn't have a care in the world. In just a few minutes, he would shatter her entire world. Perhaps he could lie and say that Arianna had taken Lucy with her when she fled the country. There was nothing he could do to stop it, and Cadmus wouldn't be able to hold it against him. A quick glance over his shoulder dashed his hopes. Four disciples in their gray robes waited just outside the inlet. There was no going back now.

Lucinda shot a beaming smile at him. "Look what we found!" She fished around the coral before pulling a starfish from the water. Its bumpy limbs waved around as she turned it over to expose the glowing blue underbelly.

Despite his mood, Silvano couldn't help but smile at her childlike joy. "It's beautiful."

"Come sit." She patted the rocky ledge next to her. "If you're very still, you might see the purple-spotted octopus that likes to hide just there." She dipped her chin to the shaded area of the inlet full of underwater crevasses.

"What, no lobster friends today?"

"They don't like the shallow water very much. It would be too easy for a hungry human to come and snatch them up."

Silvano reached over and pulled a strand of seaweed from her coiled hair. "Lucy, there's something I need to talk to you about." His voice cracked.

"What is it?" Her large green eyes peered up at him—completely innocent and trusting. He couldn't bear to break her heart.

He had no choice.

He took a shaking breath. "You know how there were some people who weren't happy that I was anointed Miestryri?" She nodded, and he continued, "Well, Head Magi Cadmus came to help me. He and his disciples have been working hard to unite our country."

"So it would be safe for me, right?"

Silvano swallowed the bile that burned his throat. He was supposed to protect her and keep her safe. How could he turn her over to a man he despised? "Exactly. I wanted it to be safe for everyone. Our people deserve that."

"What's wrong?"

"There are many ways for someone to serve their country. Cultors grow our food. Armises protect us. The small council makes decisions to improve our lives. Sometimes, the way we want to do things isn't the best way, and we need to make hard choices. Do you understand what I'm saying?"

Her face scrunched up in confusion. "Sil, you're scaring me."

"Now that the job is done, it's time for them to go back to Order Headquarters and you... You are going to go with them." He could see the moment it dawned on her, and the devastated look on her face would forever be seared into his memory. Before he could change his mind, he motioned for the disciples to approach. Lucinda clung to his legs in a claw-like grip. "I'm sorry, Lucy. I love you."

"Please don't send me away! I promise I'll be good. I won't run away from my tutors anymore. I'll do whatever you tell me. Please!"

He closed his eyes, as if not seeing her would somehow shield him from her grief. "I'm so sorry, Lucinda."

"Sil, please!"

The disciples pried her arms from his legs and dragged her away. She screamed and thrashed like a seal caught in a fisherman's net, but she couldn't break free, no matter how she struggled. Glass screeched in alarm. The dolphin chased after the disciples, slamming into them and whipping them with his tail. He transformed from a gentle familiar into a savage in a desperate bid to save her. One of the disciples went under, and Glass swam on top of him, holding him down. The nearest disciple cried out and rushed to help. She drew her sword and, without hesitation, plunged it through Glass's skull.

The water ran red.

Lucinda's anguished cry was unlike anything he'd ever heard. His heart shattered. He collapsed in the water, not caring that the sharp coral lacerated his hands. The disciples dragged Lucinda out of sight. A sob wrenched free from his throat, and tears flowed freely down his cheeks.

He curled up in the water and wept.

***

Hours passed before Silvano made his way back to the castle, still covered in Glass's blood. He shrugged off his guards' concerns. He couldn't be bothered to care. He was numb. For once, he was grateful to feel nothing.

Jax met him at the top of the steps and rested a hand on his shoulder. "You did the right thing."

"Then why does it feel like I've made the biggest mistake of my life?" Silvano whispered. The full force of what he'd done slammed into him, and the words came rushing out. "They killed him, Jax. They killed her familiar. He was just trying to save her. Her screams…"

Jax looked like he was struggling for words. "We all have to make sacrifices for the greater good."

Silvano shook his head. "Family shouldn't be one of them."

Head Magi Cadmus walked up, flanked by twelve disciples. It was the only thing that kept Silvano from attacking him. "Miestryri, I had begun to wonder if you weren't coming to say goodbye."

"Where is Lucinda?"

"Asleep. She was having a fit, so our Healer decided to give her a tonic to sleep."

"You drugged my sister?" His hands balled into fists. Disciples or not, Silvano was seconds away from pummeling the man. He wanted to tear Cadmus to pieces with his bare hands.

Cadmus appeared nonplussed. "It was for her own comfort and safety, I assure you."

Silvano closed in on him and glared down at the man. "I would hope her safety is a priority for you."

"As long as loyalty is a priority for you." A smile played on his lips. That, more than anything, terrified Silvano. One step out of line and Cadmus would take out the punishment on her. He couldn't risk it. As much as it killed him to submit, Silvano backed away and nodded. Cadmus continued, "I sent a team of disciples and a Veniet across the border to track your other sister, Arianna. She won't get far before she's captured."

"Thank you, Head Magi." The words were bitter on his lips, and he sank into a reluctant bow.

"Excellent. Well, it has been an absolute pleasure working with you." Cadmus led his disciples down the steps and began to climb into a waiting carriage. "Oh, I almost forgot. I left a present for you in the throne room. Consider it a parting gift, from one friend to another."

Silvano watched as the carriages rolled down the street, wondering which carried Lucinda. She was being taken from the only home she'd ever known to be raised by strangers. Would anyone at Order Headquarters give her comfort? Would she ever forgive him? He waited until the carriages had disappeared beyond the horizon before trudging into the castle, his heart torn from his chest.

Jax walked by his side as he entered the throne room to see what surprise Cadmus had left for him.

Lucan waited, gagged and bound hand and foot, lying on his side.

Jax opened his mouth to call for the guards, but Silvano held up a hand to silence him. Silvano crouched next to him on the floor. All the rage that had been building unleashed in a maelstrom of emotion. So much of his suffering had been caused by this man's meddling. And now, he could have his revenge.

Silvano looped a finger through the gag and pulled it free. Whatever Lucan saw on his face caused his eyes to widen, and he made a pathetic attempt to scoot away. "Miestryri, please. Mercy!"

"So it's 'Miestryri' now, is it?"

"Whatever you want, I'll give it to you. Secrets, money, loyalty. It's yours. Mercy!"

"How positively brazen to think you'll get any mercy from me." Silvano chuckled under his breath. He leaned down, removing the bonds at Lucan's ankles, then pulled the advisor to his feet. With a vicious shove, he pushed him toward the door. "Let's go for a walk. The cliffs are beautiful this time of day."

About the Author

Bethany Hoeflich is the author of the Dreg Trilogy. She lives in Central Pennsylvania with her husband, three children and an assortment of furry (and scaly) creatures. Monday through Friday, Bethany is at the mercy of the sadistic whims of her scatterbrained muse, feverishly churning out the words for her next novel. On the weekends, Bethany wrestles narwhals, participates in competitive taco-eating competitions and visits alternate dimensions through a rift in her stereotypically dark and spooky basement.

www.bethanyhoeflich.com

Made in the USA
Lexington, KY
25 November 2019